FROM GUNPOWDER

J. E. PACE

CHAPTER 1

I never forget a name. Or a voice. In fact, I'll remember the color of your nails when you put the clipboard down, the shape of your knuckles, the turn of your ring, the freckles along your arm.

A bizarre talent that didn't have much room for growth in the dentist's office where I used to work (and I thank my stars every day that I wasn't the dentist herself because—all those mouths—I never would have forgotten them; and some of them, well, you kind of want to forget).

As for *my* name. Macie. Macie Greene.

Nice to meet you.

Maybe I would have worked in that dentist's office forever, remembering names and filing X-rays, if my boss, Rachel, who also became my best friend, hadn't had to go and die. After that, it didn't take long for me to quit—the whole place just felt so empty. I drifted from one office to another, looking for a place where I fit just right. Which started to feel like nowhere.

And then my husband left too. He didn't die, in case that was unclear. He went to find himself. Because himself was not, apparently, in the life and house we'd been trying to build together for the past ten years.

After that, I got a call. A little spot with the police department had opened up. Receptionist. Same thing I'd been doing, only with uglier nails and dirtier knuckles now handing back the clipboard.

A temp job. Rachel's sister-in-law, Kate—she was having a baby, her fourth or fifth—needed someone to fill in at the police station. And, well, I needed a spot to fill. Somewhere, anywhere. With my dead friend, and dead marriage, and dead hopes of ever having a family. After all, I was pushing forty. Short, bobbed hair, a little round in the way a lot of guys didn't trip over themselves to get a piece of. That was okay, because after my marriage went up in flames, I wasn't so sure I wanted to be the piece guys went for anyway.

What I really wanted was to drown in my work— a thing that was, that *is,* difficult to do when I'm working as a temp secretary and I know the normal gal will be back in a couple months to reclaim her job.

I do my best to drown in it anyway. My paperwork is always done, perfectly filed. I even make a new organizational system for the active cases on the computer. It isn't enough. I still have moments without work to do, moments when too many thoughts, too many memories crowd my brain. In order to push them out, I start sketching some of the hands that come across my desk.

From the chipped red fingernails (hooker most likely) to the bruised purple middle finger (no idea) to the calloused fingertips (guitar player) to the knuckles lined in oil and grime (machinist) to the brown, slender fingers of Officer Brandt to the stubby, beefy paws of Sergeant Black to impeccably clean nails of Chief Sanders. And then one man. Broad, square nails. Almost like a kid had drawn them up in geometry class. Normally manicured, but today that fat pinkie finger has a sliver of brown under one nail. Dirt maybe, but probably not. Not here. Not today.

Question is, was it his blood or somebody else's?

Not my job to answer. But in my break I draw that hand, ignoring the sandwich that sits beside me, ignoring the bustle and sound around me, ignoring

the laughing and curses that are the police department—all my focus on the arc of that pinkie, that
pinkie that I want to get just right. A voice rumbles
behind me and I half jump out of my chair, stabbing
the lower half of one of the knuckles I'm drawing in
the process.

"Ms. Greene," the chief bellows like I'm not half a
foot away.

"Sir?"

He leans then, bald head tipping forward, the
only hairs in sight a few that straggle from his ears.
"I'd like a word with you. In my office."

He doesn't snap his fingers, but it has that vibe.
I tuck the notebook in my bag and trudge
after him.

By the time I get to his office, he's already seated
and looking all zen as though he wasn't hovering
over me just two minutes ago.

"Sir?" I repeat.

"Didn't realize you were an artist."

I wasn't really and say so.

"Then what, exactly, do you call that drawing in
your bag?"

Boredom. But I don't say that. "Just a sketch, sir."
And then I wonder—maybe I'm not allowed to draw
the clientele that pour through the doors of this
department. "Am I in trouble?"

The chief doesn't answer. "Drawn from memory?" he asks.

"Yeah, I—"

"And with precision."

"My brain kinda does things with precision," I reply.

He nods.

I'm still not sure if I'm in trouble or not.

"What else does your brain do?" he asks.

I look at the walls, his desk clear of everything except one of those huge daily calendars. "I guess it remembers."

"And what," he says, leaning forward, hands steepled in a way that definitely makes me feel like I'm in trouble, "does it remember?"

"Names mostly," I say. "And the voices that go with them. Faces sometimes. And—" I point to my bag. "—hands obviously. Stuff like that."

He leans back, the steeple of his fingers grazing his chin, like the tip of a gun he's forgotten to set aside.

"Name them," he says.

"Who?" I ask.

"Each person who's crossed your desk today."

That's an easy one. Thursdays are always slow. The lady who smelled like a poodle and sounded like one too with that high, barking cough. Too many nights on the street. Red fingernails. Wine and blood. Janine Jakovsky. The other woman who wasn't a woman at all. Patsy (just Patsy), she called herself, well maybe himself, since he only does drag a few nights a week. A hobbyist. He was brought in drunk and in full costume. Hot pink everywhere—nails, lips, cheeks, dress, shoes. Not an accent piece in the whole getup. Time to up the game and get a blue purse or belt or boots or something (Thinks the dowdy lady whose husband left her. Maybe I should take the fashion advice, not give it.) Patsy's voice tipped into the stratosphere until he mumbled under his breath (which he did a lot). Then it was a rumbling, hissing sound, a leak from a gas stove.

Two more men. Bill Menard and Tyler Smithson. Plain enough. T-shirts, jeans, baritones. Though one sang more while the other gurgled like he'd had a cold for ten years. One here to pick up a daughter; the other, a son.

And then, bloody pinkie—the inspiration for my staggering work of artistic genius, drawn out on a notebook with lined paper. Classy, right? Just like me. Anyway, his name was Clarence Turone, and that was all of them.

The room goes quiet after that. Seven clicks of the second hand on the clock.

"You're hired," he says, both hands tapping the desk, just before the eighth second strikes.

"With all due respect, sir, I already am. Hired, I mean."

"Not like this you're not." And then the smile. Almost like an eel with his thick, dark lips. But only if eels could be really happy and kind of sweet.

"Victoria," he says, clicking a button on his phone. "Send a message to Tad. He's getting an assistant."

CHAPTER 2

The body is covered, scene taped off. Everything in order and about to be shuffled and filed away. The house looks like crap. Not to speak ill of the dead or anything, but dude had about forty-seven cats and not a litter box in sight. And it kind of shows. Beneath the dresser, a new litter of kittens was mewing.

Tad didn't notice any of this. Or maybe he noticed all of it. It was hard to tell. His eyes flit over the scene with a vacant look, his fingers tapping soundlessly around the room, touching everything. A job that I don't envy.

You've seen *Psych* maybe. Or *Monk*. Hyper observant, loveable weirdos, working for the cops—assigned the job to see all the things the police don't see. Tad was like that. With one crucial difference.

He can't see a thing. And so he touches and listens and smells. While I watch. The new girl, sent to be his eyes.

He isn't too happy about it.

He grunts something to me about the time and circumstances of the death, and I look at the body under the sheet.

Which is, to say the least, a step up in my career. From temp receptionist to almost detective. Working with a man who wears freaking cufflinks to a crime scene. I glance sideways at the fitted suit, the shoes polished till you can see the lights reflect in them. Me, I'm wearing jeans and a t-shirt, my hair in a super short half pony tail that is a little crooked on the top of my head. As basic as you can get. Per my usual. But seriously, there's blood on the floor. I didn't realize that made for a black tie event.

"So what are we looking for?" I ask.

"You're looking," he replies. Which almost makes me laugh, but also annoys me, because he knows what I mean.

"Okay," I say. "What am I looking for? And you, sniffing for, or whatever?"

He doesn't turn to me. Normally I'd say that that was just a thing blind guys didn't do, but in this case it was definitely a slight.

"I'm sniffing for things the seeing miss," he says. "So I don't know what you're looking for."

I rifle through a few papers on the desk. I wear gloves. Tad has special permission not to. Bills, still in their envelopes, a grimy takeout menu along with a napkin, folded and unused.

"Bunch of bills he hasn't paid," I say.

"Yeah, cops already know he was hopelessly in debt. They don't think this was about that."

I look at the sheet-covered body.

Then what is it about, I wonder. I have to remind myself that I'm not really a detective. Just a used-to-be-temp with a photographic memory, a steady sketching hand, and a good ear. I look around at the scene, allow the details to blur, and listen. A few of the cats mew. Several kittens are under the bed. Outside a squirrel chatters. One of the cops slurps his coffee. And then the phone rings.

Tad and I both jump. The cop looks up as the answering machine picks up. "Didn't even know those things still existed," he says.

It is odd.

"Hey," a slightly accented voice says on the machine. High tenor or low alto—not clearly male or female. "Missed you last night. Call me."

"Well, someone's gonna be disappointed," the junior officer says, trying to coax the kittens out with a bit of bagel housing a chunk of cream cheese. A tiny pink tongue laps out at it, followed by a paw. Disgusting house aside, it's pretty cute.

"Did he not have a cell phone?" Tad asks.

"He did," the senior officer responds.

"Hmm," Tad says and the whole room seems to get it, though I don't.

"So," the senior cop says. "The home number was likely for someone he didn't want to be able to follow him around, someone he didn't want to contact him anywhere else. Someone he probably just wanted to meet at the apartment."

"Accent, Thai," Tad says. "Long time in the U.S. or maybe even second generation, considering how light it was."

"Girl or guy?" one of the cops asks.

"Unclear," Tad answers, tipping an ear unconsciously toward the voicemail machine, red light now flashing.

Before I can pick up the takeout menu, Kitten Cop is there, fishing the menu out of the stack. "We can run it for DNA. See what happens."

Guess my eyes aren't super necessary after all.

"Anyone hungry?" the senior cop asks, dialing the number.

I barely dodge a cat turd and realize I'm definitely not hungry. But the guys all put in an order.

"You gonna recognize that voice?" the head cop asks.

"Likely," Tad says.

The cop flips it to speaker.

A kitten weaves around my leg. I reach down and pet it.

The tenor-alto voice answers, "Hello, Thai Kitchen. How can I help you?"

Tad nods. "That's the one."

But it isn't. I can tell from the clipped consonants at the end of the words; they're not quite the same. Similar. Almost. Maybe a sibling or parent.

"No," I say as the cat settles for a nap against my shoe.

Tad turns to me, turns *on* me—the girl who was supposed to be the eyes. He can't see me, not really, but in his cheekbones and the purse of his lips, I get the idea that he's staring daggers anyway.

CHAPTER 3

The next day, there's a new temp girl at my desk. Yellow hair, yellow sweater, light eyes. I nod when I see her and she smiles, then looks back down at her phone. I wander past my old desk, not sure where to go now. Chief intercepts me and waggles a finger, telling me to follow him to his office.

"Am I fired?" I ask.

He tips his head to the side, a little bald chickadee. "Promoted," he says. "That's what happens when you're right. And you were right. The voices were from different people. We found the mother's DNA all over the crime scene. She murdered our guy after finding out that he was hooking up with her son—her teen son."

"Whoa," I say.

He nods. "Terrible story. The good news is that I'm assigning you to be Tad's new partner. He could use you on more cases than this one."

I wonder if he's told Tad about this. "So, no more receptionist work at all?"

He nods.

"And no longer Tad's assistant."

A firmer nod.

I lift an eyebrow. "That has a nice ring, but were you going to ask me if I wanted to be promoted?"

The chief laughs. "No, I wasn't." He leans forward, a serious look slipping over his face. "Would you like to be promoted to a position for which you won't need additional credentials that would allow you to work with some of the top people in the department and would triple your pay?"

I clear my throat. "I'll consider it," I say primly, trying not to give away my own smile.

He laughs, this huge belly sound that shakes his desk. I thought chiefs were supposed to be mean and gruff and stuff, but I'd hire this guy to be my grandpa any day.

He hands me a file. "Notes for your next assignment."

$\mathcal{I}$ see the mother later that day. Hear her actually. She's grumbling about a "disgusting man" to one of the detectives or a lawyer or someone. Barely an accent at all. I take a peek through the little one-way window. She's a tiny, lithe thing, gesturing wildly. And, I mean, murder was hardly the right choice, but I feel a little sorry for her anyway.

Tad glides past my new desk—now right next to his—without a word.

I settle in and pull out the folder the chief gave me. It has an address and a time. Looks like everyone survived, but the girlfriend is pressing charges, and we'll be assessing the scene. I admit that I'm a little relieved there won't be another body in the middle of the room.

I steal a glance at Tad. He's settled into his desk and I'm surprised to see him with a similar file pressed up to his face, just a couple inches from one eye. That's interesting, and it sparks a million questions. Questions that—judging from Tad's frown and the way he's deliberately angled his body away from my desk—I won't be asking today.

I lay my own file back on my desk and take out my sketchbook, drawing a couple of kittens from the last scene—a little tabby and the golden one with black markings that settled against my leg. At Rachel's dentistry we thought it was high drama the day the hygienist dropped a crown, cracked it, and put it in the patient's mouth anyway. When the patient called with horrible tooth pain, threatening to sue, Rachel had to grovel and then personally fix it. For that, the hygienist got a firm rebuke. And we all went on with our lives.

I just helped solve a murder and for that, it looks like I'll get the silent treatment. Awesome.

CHAPTER 4

By the time I arrive at the scene we're supposed to assess, Tad is wrapping up. Which means he came early.

"Basic domestic," he says. "Write the notes, will you, Macie?"

Well, at least he knows my name. "Okay," I mutter.

"After all," he says, pointing to his eyes. "That's going to be big part of your job."

And, you know, I just really didn't think that last part was necessary. I take the notes he dictates to me. Then, in a simple act of rebellion, I sketch out the room. Couple of couches. Two windows and a little bookshelf between them. A bookshelf that has no books because they've all been knocked down. One of the windows is old and painted shut. The other has been recently replaced and has a new latch, a new latch that isn't entirely turned into position.

⁂

*W*hen the chief shows up in front of our desks this time, he doesn't even bother to try to hide his smile. "Great job with that last case, you two. And, Macie, that sketch was on point. Helped us understand how the boyfriend got into the house. Glad you thought to ask her to do that, Simmons."

Tad nods, a brittle movement, then taps his fingers against a pencil on his desk, finding its bends, the sharp tip. I look at the pencil, and then at his face. He's not even trying to look at me.

⁂

*F*or the next few weeks, taking notes is all I do. No more cases come up that require my specialized services, which means that the chief asks me to tag along and take notes on various other cases. To be honest, it seems like the chief has to make up a little work to keep my job position relevant. I'm not sure if I should feel flattered or hurt. I mean, it's nice that he values me enough to keep me on, and at higher pay. But, on the other hand, *am* I relevant?

To fill the time, I take to sketching more hands. I work out the chief's dense fingers, Tad's slender ones, and the new temp receptionist with her French tips formed in perfect moons over her fingers. It's not the only look she's got going for herself either. High heels, a skinny little belt, and earrings for days. At least three of the guys have asked her out already. I mean, there aren't even that many days in the weekend. Don't guys notice this sort of thing—like, "Hey didn't I just see Bill flirting with her? Then Tom. Oh well, I'm sure I've got a shot..."

Tad's desk is a bit to my right and I try not to look that direction very often. Instead, I sketch the guy at the desk left of me, as well as each person who hands a file or note over to me. But even with all those possibilities, I have to admit that I create an awful lot of sketches with cufflinks. Tad's hands pop up from my memory at least three times in my sketchbook—our first scene together, then the domestic where he wore that simple black shirt, tight across his chest, fitted at the waist. Hands free of rings so he could tap them across every unnoticed object in the house. And the last sketch—a little made up. Not his hands as I'd seen them, but as I thought of them—long, gently curving. I slam the notebook closed.

The chief stops by my desk just as I do. He glances down at the book, then back at me. "Ms. Greene," he says, that formal authority dripping off every syllable. "They have positions in various cities for crime artists. I'd hate to lose you, but I also hate to waste your talents, and they could pay double what we can. I know Lexington is looking for a good one right now. I could send you over there with a glowing recommendation."

"You couldn't," I say, fidgeting with the notebook. "I can only draw what I've seen. People would describe someone and for all I know he'd come out looking like you. Or Brandt over there; or Sargent Black."

"Or Mr. Simmons," he adds.

"Sure," I say. "Or him." Cool as a cucumber, nothing given away. And just to prove how irrelevant that is, I flip the book open to a picture of Tad's hands and set it on the desk. But I feel the betrayal of my pulse—that stupid heart hammering against my chest.

"I wouldn't want to give you up to Lexington anyway," he says. Then, "I think we've got a case for you."

ad's not there, just a shrink they use occasionally. There's also some kind of mystic humming her way around the apartment. She tells us she's supposed to be there, that the chief hired her.

"Did he?" I hiss to the other officer—a guy named Hammond—dabbing at my nose with a tissue. The pollen count is sky high and I'm feeling it.

He shrugs. "It happens sometimes—they hire psychics and weird stuff like that. And it makes sense for this scene with all this junk." He waves his arm around at the apartment, which is decked out like it's 1975. A record player with a whole shelf full of various records—everything from Pink Floyd to nature sounds, along with a few books on enlightenment, one huge orange shag rug, and sheer curtains with beads. "Maybe they wanted an expert of some sort, though Chief didn't mention it. I texted him. We'll find out soon enough."

I lift an eyebrow. The mystic's legitimately got a crystal shoved between her boobs. Not sure that's gonna help, but who am I to tell PD how to do its job.

Our victim isn't here. Whether or not he's dead, well, that's the question. Apparently, one day he up and vanished. Quite literally, per some of the students in his "meditation circle."

But considering the amount of LSD they found from the original investigation, the good guru's trip to enlightenment may have been a trip of a different sort.

"Where's Tad?" I ask Officer Hammond. He's gazing through a series of dreamcatchers that have hung long enough unattended to be coated in spiders threading through the macramé with their own webs. I wonder if they still catch dreams or just juicy bugs. Looking at them, I sneeze. My eyes are starting to itch and I pull out another tissue.

"He's got another job today," Officer Hammond says. "It's too bad."

Got that right. This would have been the perfect place for his bloodhound nose and those tapping fingers.

"Have the dogs been in?"

He nods. "Yeah, first time we searched. Truth is, this place smells like drugs from floor to ceiling, like that's all they ever did. The dogs found a couple good caches but the whole place reeks of it."

I sniff, but only smell my own clogged sinuses.

The mystic shooshes us. Legit. Like she's a librarian and not a woman clad in sheer flowing clothes (a lot like the curtains if I'm being honest) and sharp phallic crystals dangling from every orifice, along with several extra piercings from which things can also dangle. She's humming a tuneless sort of chant or melody.

Hammond is trying not to look at the red thong that is visible beneath her white pants—an act of gallantry and will on his part, if I do say so myself. And I'm pretty sure the shrink has fallen asleep.

Her humming gets louder, higher. I can't say it's an unpleasant sound, and I find my mind wandering with the music. Air and vibration, soothing. No wonder the shrink is asleep. In fact, I notice that Hammond is starting to drop off too—his head bobbing down, snapping up, then bobbing and snapping. He must have picked up an extra shift the night before.

I guess I kind of miss having Tad on scene. At least he managed to stay awake. And then I notice the mystic looking at me—her voice steady, soft, almost like a charm. Her fingers run along a pendant held in her palm. A rhythm—the way my grandma used to do with her rosary beads, though this isn't a bead, just another crystal.

I close my eyes, surprised at how tired I feel as her voice hums and dips against my brain. My grandmother's hands flowing along one bead after another. A chant, a prayer. The mystic's voice. Like crystal gone soft. Turning to liquid.

My eyes snap open, but she doesn't see. She's no longer cross-legged on the floor, although her crystal has been abandoned where she was sitting. I squint, trying to force the fog from my mind. It's not a crystal at all, but a vial; and the woman has crawled to a segment of the wood paneling in the wall, then moved it, just like a door.

I rub my eyes. Yup, she's still there. As silently as possible, keeping my lashes lowered over most of my eyes, I touch Hammond's arm. He doesn't move. I poke it harder. Nothing. Finally, I pinch a skinny little bit of neck flesh tight between my fingers.

He starts, hand going swiftly and silently for his gun, without even establishing full consciousness. I step back so I don't get shot, hold a finger to my lips, signaling for him to be quiet.

He blinks like a week-old kitten. I tip my head to

the side, pointing. He's struggling to follow, but I've got to give it to him; he doesn't make a sound. After a million minutes, or maybe one, he slowly turns his head, hand still on the gun in his holster. Eyes widening, he sees it—the man in the hidden panel embracing sheer curtain pants lady.

Hammond clears his throat.

We've found our missing person.

The path to enlightenment, it seems, is paved with drugs, hypnosis, and a messy, expensive divorce brought on by a red-thonged, crystal-breasted affair. Apparently, when faced with potential child support, it's just easier to disappear.

"Should have brought the dogs again," I say as Hammond leads the unhappy lovers to the squad car.

"Should have brought Tad," he says. "He would have smelled that in a second."

"Then he would have fallen asleep first," the woman says. "Obviously."

Hammond turns to me, just in time to see me shove a tissue into my pocket. "Well, then, good thing her nose is dead."

"The best," I grumble.

nd so, thanks to the torture of seasonal allergies, a dusty apartment, and my utter lack of olfactory observational skill, I win another one for the team.

Chief is humming. Hammond has a headache the size of Texas (his words, not mine). And our crystalline lovers—they're out on bail within twenty-four hours. Apparently, a little divorce fraud and an aromatic that makes everyone drowsy isn't enough to warrant more.

***

ad leaves a message on my phone. I listen on my drive home, leaning toward the sound of his voice. "Rumor has it you've saved the day again." It doesn't sound like he's happy about it. I lean back, pressing my head against the seat of the car.

***

hen I arrive at work the next day, there's a little message on my desk with a piece of chocolate. I glance at Tad's desk. It's empty; he hasn't even gotten to work yet.

Slowly, almost sneakily, I slit the envelope open. It's a little card with a flower on front and a phone number inside with the word 'Sal' scrawled across it —those three little letters taking almost the entire card.

Sal. A name that was short, I'd been told, for Salvador. He's just arrived at his own desk, looking fresh and pressed and buff and amazing. Per his usual. Yeah, I'd noticed him. Who wouldn't? He's a big hunk of man-flesh, the type people hire for bachelorette parties to strip off their fake police clothes. I blush slightly at the thought. I'm relieved to note that his uniform is definitely not easily strippable, and then I blush again at that thought. Anyway, he's a big dude. Hazelnut skin, chocolate eyes, full head of black hair. Yeah, people would definitely hire this guy for a party, if he wasn't here being an actual police officer instead. He catches my stare, and winks.

Later that night, I call him and he asks if I'd like to meet him for coffee on Saturday. I haven't been on a single date since Alex left. Captain Biceps seems like a big shift, and a good place to start. I'm always up at the crack of dawn anyway, thinking and worrying. It can't be much harder to wake up and meet an attractive man for my caffeine fix instead. Right?

CHAPTER 6

Wrong.

Per my usual, I wake up worrying, and per my usual, I'm up before the sun. I already feel jittery, but I start brewing coffee before I realize I'm going to be drinking even more coffee soon. I spill the first cup on my first blouse—my favorite blue one. Then have to dig another out of my drawer. It could really use an iron, but I just throw it in the dryer with a wet washcloth, hoping that in fifteen minutes, it will be passable. Sitting there in my bra with coffee still spilled on the table, I almost text Sal to cancel. I hold the phone in my hand, tapping out an excuse, which I quickly erase.

This will be good for me, I tell myself.

And it is. My shirt looks fine. My shoes even match. And Sal and I—we laugh, tell jokes, talk about work. Sal fills me in on all the points of gossip. Anderson's wife is a stewardess and you can always tell when she's gone because he works practically the entire time. Long's got three kids, but no husband, and she won't talk about it. Chief's a teddy bear most of the time, except for the days he's a grizzly. Those are bad days. Hammond is dating Schwartz, but first dated a waitress from the place down the street. Nelson went after the new temp first, and now there's a bit of a fight with Richards over it.

"Yeah, seems like they kind of lost their minds over her," I say.

"Not my type," Sal says like he's trying to reassure me, even though I'm pretty sure I wasn't asking for reassurance. Was I? The uncertainness stops a couple of the follow-up questions I want to ask, and I catch myself wondering if Tad would have noticed the dropped thread of conversation. Sal doesn't.

He tells me about his job with the Community Oriented Policing (the acronym is literally COP), which deals with problems like homeless people and ugly lawns. Not exactly glamorous, but important for a city.

"That's just about everybody," I say casually. "Except Tad. What's his deal?"

"You probably know better than I do," Sal says.

"He's a blind genius, obviously. But other than that, he keeps to himself."

I nod.

"Oh," Sal says. "And Rosa."

"Rosa?" I ask, thinking she's Tad's girlfriend or something.

"I forgot Rosa. She owns this little food truck, makes the best tamales I've ever tasted. Brings them sometimes on Fridays."

"Well, if that isn't a reason to go to work," I say, relieved she isn't Tad's lover. Until I realize that that's not what I should be thinking right now. Like, it's way off track when I'm *here* with hot, hunky Sal.

"You have no idea," Sal adds, and it takes me a moment to remember where we are in the conversation. "I'll bring you one next time. You'll see."

Oh, yeah, tamales. "That sounds nice," I say.

"The only place that comes close is this little Mexican restaurant off of Dover Street. I should take you there sometime. I mean, if you want to go."

"Today?" I ask.

"You have plans?" he asks.

And I make up some plans real quick. If Rachel was still alive it'd be easy. We could go to a movie, or out for dessert. No blatant lying necessary. As it is, I have to make up a friend, and when I do, a big old welt seems to grow in my stomach. A little of it is guilt, but most of it is missing. Missing Rachel. Missing friendship.

"Yeah, can't tonight," I say. "Girls and I are going out."

As if. It's the worst lie ever, but Sal doesn't notice.

Which makes me feel even worse. But a morning-to-night date is a little too much for me right now. Kind of like the three cups of coffee I'm working on.

"I'll catch you another time, then," he says, and there's a little dimple on the left side of his grin.

I catch myself nodding. "Yeah, that would be nice."

He pecks my cheek as we leave the coffee shop, and it's more action than I've had in over a year.

CHAPTER 7

Tad and I are paired again, along with a detective named Anderson. I get the impression that Anderson is kind of a big shot. At least as big a shot as we get in a town like Swallowsville.

When we enter the house, there are bodies. Woman dead, man dead, gun on the floor by his hand. Cops are milling around. The paramedics are already gone and the coroner is about to leave, just finishing his report.

It's a case that looks like a cut-and-dried murder-suicide. Until Tad and I spot the clue at the same time—him with fingers, me with eyes. The man was holding the gun with his right hand, but has callouses only on the fingers and palm of his left hand. Tad is rubbing them as I look at the right hand. A few of the fingers are curled in, almost like a claw. Tad shuffles over and feels it, like he's giving this dead guy a hand massage. "It's stiff," he says.

"It's a corpse," Anderson answers, squatting down to the dead body's level.

"The rest of him is more supple," Tad says, prodding around like dead guy massage is totally his jam.

"If you say so," Anderson says, like he has no intention of taking any of this new information into account. Until I spot the paperwork: a doctor's appointment for a physical therapist, right there on the fridge.

Anderson sighs. "I'll check into it."

I'm honestly not sure that he really will, but when we come to work the next day, the report is on both my desk and Tad's. The suspected shooter was indeed left-handed. Prove-ably left-handed. Turns out that during his military service, he suffered from some paralysis in his right hand, making it nearly unusable. Whether he was born left-handed or not, he had been for most of his adult life.

"Guess you guys found yourselves a case," Anderson is saying, like it's the worst news he's had all day. "We'll go to that house later today to have a closer look at the scene."

Tad is holding the paper report up to his face, just about an inch away from his eye, like he's reading it. Either that or smelling it, but I'm pretty sure that wouldn't be very effective for a medical report.

"So," I begin. "You can see?"

"You think they gave me this desk so I could look pretty?" Tad asks.

"Well, that's one thing you're good at," I reply with a bit of bite in my voice.

He sets the report down. "I have one small pinprick of vision through my right eye. It's not much, but I can read and see when things are held up close. Happy?"

Nope. I feel pretty miserable, if we're being honest. I've embarrassed him, and myself. If Twitter got a hold of this, they'd roast me for being basically the most insensitive human in the entire world. "Sorry," I grumble.

He's back to the report and he doesn't look up from it, but his head kind of tips to the side, in my direction.

"'S okay," he says into the paper.

And maybe I'd focus on this little exchange for much longer if the report wasn't sitting right in front of me. A supposed murderer who killed his wife, only he couldn't have because he wouldn't have had the coordination to hold a gun in that hand. But if he didn't kill his wife, or himself, then who did?

I run a pen over my sketchbook, trying to remember the angle of the man's hand, the way the gun lay on the floor, the layout of the scene, trying to find the thing that was missing—the other person who must have been there.

The next logical choice is the wife.

Why spouses so frequently murder one another is beyond me—and this coming from a long-time unhappily married woman.

But in autopsy everything checks out with her. She couldn't have been shot at the angle she was if she did it herself. Not to mention the fact that it would have been really hard to shoot him, then herself, then put the gun near his hand like he did it. Not to mention the blood trail she would have left. Not to mention the fact that she'd know which hand was his dominant hand. Yeah, it just didn't make sense—autopsy or no.

Which leaves us to examine the angle at which the man was shot. It looks, still, like a suicide—like he was holding the gun in his right hand.

"So strange," Tad says as I hover over his desk, examining part of the report. He's holding another paper up to his eye in that way he does. And I wonder how it would be to see like that—through a pinprick of light and color. I wonder how it makes him see me, or if he even can. Not that I'll be asking anytime soon. He moves the paper down another notch, those soft, worn, perfectly proportioned fingers slipping along the thin paper.

I clear my throat.

"Allergies still bothering you?" he asks.

"Uh, no, they're okay today," I say.

He nods. "Give me a minute."

"No, I...Take your time." I turn my attention again to the pictures of the bodies. But they just make me sad, so I close my own eyes, hear everyone's voices. Sal is on the phone and bored out of his mind. Anderson mumbling away through a report, talking to himself. Most people can't hear him, much less understand the muted diction. But I can. Officer Long's got her kid on the phone again—I can hear both their voices clear as day—someone whining about Minecraft; then Long's clipped, "Don't call me again at work unless it's an emergency."

"It is," the child's voice fusses. But he's cut off from the call with a quick, "Love you. Bye." Long leans her head in her hands.

"Tough to handle momming and policing," I say.

She looks up with a half-smile. "Honestly, they're practically the same thing. Trying to get the truth out of people, stop domestic violence, keep people from stealing toys. It's all there."

I laugh.

"How old are your kids?" she asks.

I stop laughing. "Oh, um, I don't have any."

Long looks at me strangely, but before she can reply or I can blurt out something about being a godmother to my friend's kid, Tad slams the report on the desk and I jump.

"Can't find a thing," he says. "Everything here indicates he did it himself. Except that he couldn't have."

I scan the report, though I'm hardly a pro at this sort of thing. After all, I was brought on because I did a good job doodling, not because I could make great headway through a lengthy autopsy report.

"Hang on," I say, trying to skim.

Tad jabs one of those long fingers at the center of the report. "The angle, the bullet hit, everything. It all indicates he did it himself. Even the time of the murder. Unless someone came up behind him in a bear hug and held the gun in his hand..." Tad pauses.

"Which seems to implicate the wife again," I say.

"Who else is he going to let come up behind him in a bear hug?" I ask.

"That is the question," Tad murmurs, staring straight ahead.

I'm scanning the report, trying to make sense of it. "He wasn't drugged, right?"

"Correct," Tad says absently.

"So what other person would have been close to him, maybe even in the room when the wife was killed. Who could have come up behind him like that without a struggle?" I pause. "No signs of a struggle, right?"

"You can't read that report at all, can you?" Tad asks.

"In case you hadn't noticed," I said. "I'm a little self-taught at policing."

"Detectiving," he corrects. "That's more what we do."

"Okay, sure," I say.

Tad smiles. An actual smile—in my direction. "I'll walk you through it later." He makes his way to Anderson's desk and I can hear him asking about close friends or family, anyone else who might have been on scene, or involved. I gaze at him from my desk, notice the perfect shadow of stubble along his jawline.

"No fingerprints," he says when he comes back.

"No unusual DNA." He rakes his hands through the wavy brown hair and stands up. "I'm too hungry to think. Come on, Greene, let's talk about it at lunch."

My heart skips a beat. I mean, it's not exactly a lunch invitation—well, it is, but not *that* kind of invitation. More of a demand really, which needles me when I notice.

"I'm on a budget," I say, tugging a sandwich out of my purse.

"Then I'll pay. Come on."

He's distracted, barely aware of me. But a free lunch is a free lunch. And a hot guy is a hot guy. I'll eat my sandwich for dinner.

She thought I never noticed her. A common enough mistake—to think not seeing equaled not noticing. Common, but wrong. I noticed her in the earthy soft scrub of her skin—lavender and cedar. I guessed, because of that smell, that she struggled to sleep. I noticed her in the even tones of her voice—a voice used to managing more than one life at a time, a voice used to the self-effacing insults it threw at itself. I noticed her in the movement—blocky, but precise. Not a willow, but an oak. I even noticed her through the small beam of vision, which was all that I had. It allowed me to read (slowly), but not to drive; to see (barely), but not to assess. It allowed me flashes of her—the short brunette hair, freckled cheeks, green eyes—so bright and round and clear. I'd caught only one flash of these eyes on one scene when she'd been close and I'd looked at her and she at me and there they were. Her eye to mine. No makeup, at least I didn't think so. Practical, cotton clothes. The kind of clothes women bought at Costco, not the mall. But I liked them, the clothes, the lack of frill and silk. Touching her would be comfortable, a blanket or a pillow of a touch. Better than the golden pink gilding of so many women—plastics and vinyls. Nothing to settle into.

I stopped on the thought. No, I stopped the thought altogether. She was clearly not interested in a relationship—not with some blind guy she worked with, anyway. Maybe not with anyone, though Sal sauntered by her desk here and there and talked. I knew she was divorced and I could feel the prickle on her skin when she mentioned it.

Sal couldn't. He'd asked her out, bragged about a second date—a second date that Macie seemed to have forgotten about. Though she wasn't the type of woman to forget things.

They'd hired her for that—that memory. And the fingers that let it spill onto paper. Such an unimaginable skill—being able to draw the things you were also able to see.

See. A thing I'd been able to do until I was nine when my world started to blur and narrow.

My teacher reported it first, like the tattletale

that she was. I hadn't even complained about the headaches, though my mother had already begun to notice my head on the table at dinner, the bleary lines from squinting.

The night my teacher called, my mother held my chin in her hand, tilting my face up and gazing into my blue eyes. Blue. The weakest color, I would later learn—most prone to vision problems, to blindness.

I could still see my mother back then, all of her face. Dark, plump, beautifully Italian. Her curls fell forward and she squinted. I squinted back, focusing on the lines that shot from the corners of her eyes, the bend of a frown at the tip of her lips. "Can you see me?" she asked.

I nodded.

She released my chin.

That was the end of it. If my mother thought I could see, then I could see.

Until eleven months later when I started bumping into things. It was my father—Scandinavian, ghost pale, with voice to match—who finally took me to the doctor. Without a word to my mother, he took the day off, picked me up at my school, took me to my appointment, then brought me home for dinner with a diagnosis in hand.

I heard my mother crying deep into the night. But the next morning at breakfast, my father looked into my failing eyes and said, "There's more to this world than what lies on the surface."

And he was right.

As the top layer of my world dimmed, all the layers beneath opened up. Its sounds, smells, nuances, hints. Did you know that as one part of the brain shuts off the others light up?

I noticed that the soft way my father said my name and the brassy way my mother did meant the same thing, a sound of loving tenderness. I noticed that a firm 'no' from both of them meant different things. I noticed that girls made noises boys didn't, and that at first I liked boys noises better with the whoops, the slaps of their tongues and teeth, but that a few years later, I found myself preferring the sounds of girls—the laughs, the soft reaches and recalls in their voices. But maybe by that age, it wouldn't have taken blindness to notice that sort of thing.

I noticed that neither girls nor boys noticed me at all, except to mock or pity the succession of eye patches, odd glasses and surgeries that became a part of my life. By age sixteen, my sight—a generous term —was set. One beam of vision in one eye. We all— father, mother, and me—felt glad to have it. And to be done with the successions of procedures, the duty of trying to save a dying thing.

My mother fought to put me in a specialized school; my father fought against it. They compromised with a tutor who followed me around in my normal classes. Perhaps the worst compromise ever for a teenage boy.

I didn't really find myself until college. Or, well, others found me. I was, apparently, decent looking (sure, waste it on the blind guy), my mother had taught me to dress well, and by then a certain crowd enjoyed a certain fetish for the type of guy I was, or was perceived to be—a good-looking hero, just disabled enough to be a little sexy, because I was a guy who had overcome all odds. If *all odds* was confined to a lack of perfect sight.

But I rolled with it, made friends—some true, some not—found more layers in the underneaths of things, and graduated with a music history degree, which proved—for me—to be nothing more than a piece of decorative paper.

Fortunately, other things proved profitable—my ears, my fingers, the layers I could see that others missed.

Until Macie came along. Shaking up the deep layers of my life, the layers I'd begun to believe were mine alone.

CHAPTER 9

He doesn't exactly go all out for our lunch not-date. Just sloppy burgers at a cheap corner diner. The burgers make my PBJ back at the station look like fine dining. Maybe he's on a budget too, though not one that skimps on the menswear. From his tie to the spit-polished shoes, he definitely looks out of place here. Bad burger or not, I have to admit that I enjoy when he rolls up his sleeves. The muscles on his forearms actually ripple with the movement and he flips the tie over his shoulder. "Tough not to make a mess here," he says, and I nod, pushing at my burger, which has meshed with the bun into a lump of soggy grease paste.

He waves the waitress away when she brings around a pot of coffee. I figure it's because he's jittery already. I wave her back and ask for a piece of pie.

It's then that the chief calls. Tad keeps the volume of his cell low, probably because he has sensitive ears like I do. When he's done, he lowers the phone kind of slow mo.

I raise an eyebrow, a gesture that's completely lost on Tad. "So?" I say.

"Chief says our guy was in physical therapy for that hand."

"Right," I say. "We already knew that."

"Well, apparently it was going very well. He might have been well enough to use that hand and do it himself. Unless something else pops up he's going to close the case. Murder-suicide. Done and done."

I click my nails, thinking.

"Stop making that noise, please."

"Sorry."

Tad's staring at nothing, which isn't unusual, but this time it feels more like a gaze. "You still don't think he did it?" I say.

Tad shrugs. "It's not a police drama on TV. If he was in physical therapy, maybe he could've done it."

"But you don't think he did?" I press.

"New evidence means it's time to pivot." He

crumples his napkin into a ball. "But I liked our ideas better. More fun."

"Because murder-suicides are fun," I say.

"Hey, in this world, you take fun where you can get it." He smiles a little lopsided thing, and now it's my turn to gaze, just a little.

His hand brushes mine as he grabs another napkin, and a happy heat prickles along my pinky.

"He does want us to go over to the house and have one last look," Tad says. "Just in case."

I nod, remember he probably can't see it and say, "Okay." I've pushed my burger to the side and am waiting on that pie.

"You don't like it?" Tad asks and I'm surprised he's noticed my abandoned burger.

"I wish I could say I was a vegetarian or something," I reply, "but I guess greasy burgers just aren't my thing. One thing my ex *did* do well was cook."

He shrugs. "Greasy burgers are an art unto themselves. But not everyone understands art, especially women who are police artists."

"Rude," I say as the waitress drops off my pie, which doesn't look half bad. "And I'm not really a police artist. Just a girl who draws."

Tad grunts, eating no less than a quarter of his burger in one bite. Impressive.

"Just a girl who draws," he says after he's chewed

his way through a heart attack's worth of grease, starch, and protein. "So draw it. The scene."

I pull my notebook out of my bag. "Truth is, I already did."

He wipes his hands on a napkin, holds the picture up to his point of vision. I've drawn the kitchen and hall with crude sketches of the husband and wife as I remember them lying, along with a sketch of how I imagined them standing before the shooting. "Not bad. Now add someone. Behind the husband. Who would it be? How would they get there? Why no signs of struggle?"

I sketch out another picture, this one with the husband still standing, a man behind him, his hand wrapped around the husband's hand, forcing him to hold the gun. It's not a bad theory.

Tad leans down, his eyes nearly touching the paper. "Could have been a woman too," he says.

"Would she have had the strength?" I ask.

"Would she have needed it?" he answers. "If there was no struggle."

Skeptically, I add long hair and curves to my sketch, so it looks like she and the husband are doing a sexy slow dance as she forces the gun to his hand.

"See," Tad says, leaning down again to inspect my work, then polishing off his burger. "Maybe he shot his wife and wanted to kill himself, but couldn't so he insisted someone else on the scene do it."

"Right," I say. "Someone who didn't try to stop him from killing his wife, but was then happy to kill him. Not a lover then or a friend or relative—to him or the wife."

"Maybe a lover to the wife. And he got mad about it."

I tilt my head back and forth, considering. "Possibly. But why kill a guy who'll wind up in prison for the rest of his life anyway? Why put your own butt on the line like that?"

"Lover's fury," Tad answers.

"Lover's stupidity," I reply.

"Wouldn't be the first time," he says. "Not all lovers are as practical as you."

Before I can defend myself by telling him I'd definitely make a passionately stupid lover, thank you very much (except that I absolutely know that I wouldn't), he says, "Okay. Okay, how about this? Maybe the husband came in with his lover, who shot the wife. But then, the husband, completely regretful, demanded that he be shot as well. Maybe he even threatened to report the lover's part in it if he didn't get shot. But the lover didn't want to be caught for a double murder, so she came up behind him and used his own hand to shoot him."

"Sure, sure," I say. "Or maybe it was a clinically insane sister who stopped taking her meds."

"Typical," Tad says, a grin tugging at his mouth. It's cute, really cute.

The stories get wilder from there. By the time the chief calls again we're onto a twisted and jealous mob boss who's been seducing and blackmailing the both of them.

Tad's still mid-laugh when he answers the phone. "Sir," he says. And then the smile fades, like they do when you're on the phone with your boss. I close my eyes to remember the look of it, catch the sound of his voice.

"Thank you, sir. We'll let you know."

CHAPTER 10

We take my car back to the house where the husband and wife had lain, paling on the floor.

They've found an extra phone with some of the husband's—Phillip's—things. A secret phone. Anderson is getting the transcripts and the chief wants me to have a look at them.

"A look?" I say to Tad.

He shrugs.

We arrive just as Anderson unlocks the door.

The house smells like lemon and bleach. Their bodies are all cleaned up now, not a trace of murder or suicide or anything except pure domestic bliss anywhere to be found.

Like, for real.

I hadn't noticed as much when there were two

bodies on the floor, but the house is filled with photos and matching dinnerware and even two champagne glasses inscribed with their wedding date. Add to that the fact that there was no history of domestic violence. No history of problems with the law at any point. No calls from the neighbors—in fact several of them are clearly grieving and have left flowers at the door. Nothing at all to indicate something deadly was about to erupt between them.

"You ready for this?" Anderson asks, handing me a transcription of the texts on their phones. "On top are the texts from the regular phones, at the bottom of the pile are the ones from the extra phone—the hidden one we found. We'll get the voice recordings for voicemails back at the station."

I read through the dialogue of the first several pages, and—to be honest—the only thing criminal about it is how boring the texts are. Just normal married stuff. "Can you pick up a loaf of bread on your way home?" Or, "Getting the dog groomed on Friday." A picture of her manicure. A funny meme about politics.

"I'm not even sure we'll need to listen to the phones if that's all it is."

"It isn't," Anderson says.

I nod, wandering through the kitchen as I sift through the texts. Except for their missing bodies, nothing has changed in the house since they were killed. Ice cream bowls in the sink, rinsed but unwashed—almost like, well, they ate it together. I set the papers down for a minute and open the cupboard. There's legit a set of "Mr." and "Mrs." mugs, front and center. I look at Tad, who's not looking back, obviously. Instead, he's feeling his way along the clean countertop, eyes completely closed.

"I think they were happy," I say, reaching up to touch a mug and stopping myself, then gathering up the papers with the transcripts, burying my head in the cheerful normalcy of their lives.

Tad nods, staring, his head tilted, listening, his fingers tapping through a stack of letters that he's found.

And then I see it—the first text of a naked woman. They've taken care to print it clearly for me. I wish they hadn't.

"Found it, did you?" Anderson says, sniggering at my blush.

"What is this?" I ask.

"The transcripts from the third phone—the one we found with the husband's things."

"I don't want to look at these," I say, turning to the next page—a pair of mostly exposed breasts.

"And I don't want to look at stinky corpses as often as I do," Anderson replies.

Tad has stopped to listen to the two of us, leaning toward our conversation.

"But why?" I ask. "What good will it do?"

"Because we need to know if this is one woman, or many. And if it is one woman, is it his wife?"

I catch Tad smiling and trying to hide it—that half lift of his mouth.

"So you need to know if this secret phone is a bunch of perverted porn, or just his wife sending him, uh, pictures?"

"Yup," Anderson says. "And you're the best candidate for the job."

I'm not so sure about that one. I bet plenty of the officers at the station would be capable of (and happy to) do a little breast matching.

"If it's a bunch of women," Anderson is saying, "then one of them might have gotten mad enough to come kill the two of them. If not…"

"…then, just a happy couple," Tad finishes for him.

"Very happy," Anderson replies.

I roll my eyes. Then take a deep breath, looking closely at the pictures. It really isn't my thing. She's got all sorts of poses—some full body and full nude, others just a piece of herself—a leg, a breast, scantily clad, barely there or barely covered. A stiletto. A bralette. I realize that as I flip through the images,

I'm coming to think of *them* as *her.* One person. They seem to match. Or is it just a bias, an inclination to hook headless body parts into a nameless human? Clearly, the full body frontals are her. I pause in a moment of pity for this woman—trying to connect with her husband, never imagining that several police detectives and a stranger of a woman would be going through them. I take a deep breath, noting her shape, her dimensions—the same way I would with a hand—measuring them with my mind, adjusting the scale for different pictures.

Anderson is peering over my shoulder.

"I thought this was my job," I snap and he backs off, laughing.

"Give the poor woman some dignity," I grumble.

"One woman?" he asks.

I don't answer, not yet. "Anybody got a pencil?"

Tad hands me one. I draw graph lines over one of the frontals. Do a little calculation, mutter, "We never did it this way in math class."

"I might have paid more attention if we had," Anderson says. "Probably be a freaking math genius."

I bite back my comment about that.

Tad has turned from both of us and is sifting through papers on the table—a stack in a little box labeled 'junk mail.'

"They're her," I say finally. "Or someone with

exactly the same measurements as she had. And same coloring. And this little birthmark on the hip above her left thigh. Which seems unlikely."

"So," Tad says, still not bothering to turn toward the pictures. "Just a happy couple."

"Seems that way," I say.

"Lucky guy," Anderson adds.

"You mean the dead dude?" I ask.

"I mean before that."

"Seriously, Anderson?" Tad says.

Anderson sighs. "Just trying to keep it light. If you don't, these things get to you."

And they did. And they were. I rip my eyes away from the dirty pictures, the matching mugs, the cute photo in the corner, the 'Gather' sign above the kitchen table. The relics of love and connection that bombard me from every edge of the room.

Anderson is still stealing glances at the transcripts. I flip the papers over and look down, thinking. Notice a dog dish on the floor. It has—I'm not kidding—a monogram of the dog's initials on the front and a picture of the couple with the dog on the back. A poodle of some sort. Was there no end to the loving cheesiness of these people?

"Who took the dog?" I ask, remembering the text about the groomer.

Anderson looks up, then down when I point to

the dish.

Tad turns to me sniffing the air like he, himself, is the dog. "How did I miss that," he mutters. "It's faint, but..."

"Maybe poodles don't shed a lot," I say. "Plus, I have the feeling they kept it pretty clean. So...Where is it?"

Anderson shakes his head. "I don't know. There wasn't a dog here when we arrived—after the shots got reported by a neighbor. So it could have run off or been shot as well."

"I would have smelled dog corpse for sure," Tad says.

"Maybe outside," Anderson says. "We'll have a look. Dogs get shot on a surprising number of these cases."

"Because they're the biggest threat," I murmur.

"Bingo," Anderson says.

"Did the neighbors hear the dog barking?" Tad asks. "Or three shots?"

"We'll find out," Anderson says, jotting things down on a pad.

"Or the dog could have been taken beforehand so it wasn't here at the time. As a coincidence. Or not," Tad says, fingering an envelope he's pulled from the pile and holding it up to his reading eye. "Maybe even taken by the person who shot them."

"Sure," I say. "Like a crazy mob boss."

Tad raises his eyebrows and the gesture looks strange above the mail he's reading.

"A family member, I'd guess," he answers.

"Why would a family member take it?" I ask. "Why would they take the dog and then brutally murder their relatives?"

"It wasn't brutal," Anderson says. "Pretty run of the mill, to be honest."

"That's not what I—"

"Because," Tad interrupts, waving the letter. "This couple was about to get rich."

I grab the letter out of his hand, skim my way through the legal mumbo jumbo about estate and last will and Mrs. Cooper Jones—a lady who'd left them some money apparently. I scan all the way down to the bit about property stocks, bonds—all that stable planning stuff my ex-husband hated to worry about. "They never say how much you inherit in these letters," I say, still not satisfied. "It could be twelve bucks."

"Mrs. Cooper Jones was a wealthy socialite. Haven't you heard of her?"

"Yeah, wealthy socialites and I hang in the same circle."

Tad purses his lips—his equivalent of an eye roll. "She was on the news several times, always doing charity events. People loved her. She died recently. And," he pauses. "It looks like she was related to the happy couple."

"I wonder if they were her only benefactors," Anderson says, reading over my shoulder.

"If they were and others weren't, that's more than enough for a decent motive," Tad adds.

"You think a relative came over, took their dog, and killed them, making it look like the husband did it?" I ask.

"I think," Tad says, holding the paper up to his eye, "that not a single other letter in this pile is open. Look."

Anderson and I shuffle through. Sure enough, only that one is open, slit carefully along the fold so as to be almost unnoticeable. And then stuck in a pile of junk mail.

"I'll call the chief," Detective Anderson says.

I take a picture of the room with my mind, different than the one I took before, more than the layout, the positions of the bodies. This time I notice the ice cream bowls, the matching mugs, the abandoned dog dish. And then I wish I hadn't because now I can't un-see it. This life I'd wanted, this beautiful togetherness that most people wish for and don't get. Gone up in two (maybe three) flashes of gunfire.

CHAPTER 11

The report comes back. No dead dog in the yard or neighborhood. Not even a poop turd. No neighbor who remembers hearing barking, or three shots. No one who saw the dog run through the neighborhood. Nothing.

Not only that, but they were indeed the only benefactors to the wealthy Mrs. Cooper and not only that, she left her grandson—the dead husband in our case—a million and a half dollars in assets.

I whistle low. Tad holds the report to his eye. When he sets it down he tip tap tips his fingers against it.

"So," I begin. "Do we have a list of relatives who might be upset about that?"

"We're not detectives," he answers.

And, you know, I'd honestly kind of forgotten. I

nod, then remember he can't see that and give a ladylike grunt. *Nice, Macie.*

"Just observers," he mumbles, talking to himself. As he says it, Detective Anderson saunters over and drops a drive on Tad's desk. "Voicemail recordings," he says when I look over. "Chief wants you both to listen to them."

"Are you going to question the relatives?" I ask.

He nods. "Leave it to you two to take a cut-and-dried murder-suicide and make it into a full-blown investigation."

Tad clenches his jaw. I note the ripple of the muscles along it.

"Usually I save you guys a lot of investigation time," Tad says.

"Usually," Anderson answers.

I look between the two of them. "If someone else killed them, isn't that important to know?" I ask.

Anderson doesn't answer, just motions down the hall. "Room three is open. Should have good sound. He tips his head down the hall. I gather up my laptop and Tad grabs his cane. Tap tap tap down the hall.

"Usually?" I ask when he's closed the door.

"Sometimes I find things," he says with a shrug. "It makes the investigation go longer and ticks those guys off."

"And?" I say as he swings down onto a chair,

laying the cane behind his feet—the most graceful movement imaginable. "You stop the bad guys?"

"It makes the investigation go longer," he repeats.

"But you stop the bad guys?" I repeat.

"So far, if I notice something that seems troubling, that lengthens out the investigation…well, so far the outcome hasn't changed a single case. Whatever they thought at the beginning is where they wind up. At least with those cases."

"And he's mad because he thinks this will be the same."

"Yup," he answers as I set my laptop up, connecting it to the speakers.

"Will it?" I ask, pressing a button.

"Maybe," he answers.

"You think it was a murder-suicide?" I ask as the window with the little play button opens.

"No," he says. "But what I think doesn't really matter."

"You think a relative killed them?"

"I think they didn't kill each other. That's all."

I want to ask why he's so sure, so confident. I want to ask if he's ever had a Mr. and Mrs. matching mug set, if it's ever gone all wrong. Instead I hit play and the messages begin.

The woman from the groomer. The dog is done and beautiful. The woman's voice sings the information onto the voicemail, but I can tell she's taken a few too many smoke breaks in her life.

Another woman's voice about coffee the next day.

A man's about pickle ball.

Two spams regarding a car warranty and a one million dollar Amazon purchase they better call to stop.

One dentist appointment. I feel a slight pang at the receptionist's voice. JoAnne—the receptionist for Dr. Icar—a nice guy. JoAnne has been working for Dr. Icar for ages. I think of Rachel, of Aiden her husband, of their little girl. It's been just over a year since Rachel died.

"Except for that sexy phone, this is the most basic couple ever," Tad says, interrupting my thoughts.

I shake my head as the next message clicks on. An older lady. Hard to understand her name because her dog barks just before she starts speaking, but she wants one of them to call her about her house. She's been hearing sounds in her kitchen wall. Thinks a raccoon might be stuck there.

Tad creases his forehead. "A renter?"

"Sounds like it," I say.

The line of recording runs out.

"So that's it."

"No siblings calling," Tad responds as we walk into the hall. "Or any other relatives either."

"Maybe," I say. "We don't know about coffee lady, or pickle ball guy, or really anyone."

"They didn't sound like relatives." He taps along with his cane. "Wonder if they've pulled up any names."

Detective Anderson butts in, turning the corner. I swear it was like he'd been waiting for us. "Anything interesting?"

"Just an auto warranty about to expire," Tad answers sarcastically.

Anderson sighs. "Guess we'll have to drag you two along to talk to the relatives. First one's this evening. Six o'clock."

So there are relatives. I really want to say, "Aha!"

But Tad is looking annoyed. "You know I don't work nights."

"Evening," he replies. "And if you can't, then I guess Macie can come alone."

Tad's cheek tightens again.

"I'm sure you could ask her for a ride if you'd like."

"Keep any other interviews to days, please," Tad replies, a forced politeness in his voice. "I know for you it doesn't matter, but for some of us it does."

Anderson smiles in a way that is mostly smirk. "See you tonight."

"You mean, 'this evening,'" Tad corrects.

"Of course I do," Anderson says, and then trots down the hall.

Tad sighs.

"Why not nights?" I ask. I'm picturing a lover falling into Tad's toned arms, the cuff links dropping to the table beside him.

"Really, Macie?" he asks.

I stare at him and he must see my clueless face through his pinpoint of vision because he says, "Buses don't run after six and Uber gets expensive."

I take in a slight breath.

"Streetlights throw me off and it's easy to trip."

"Oh...yeah—" I begin.

"But, honestly, thanks for thinking of me as normal for a second. That jerk doesn't." He tips his chin in the direction of Anderson's desk. "He set it for six on purpose."

I remember what Sal said about Anderson always working extra when his wife is away.

"I'll give you a ride," I say.

"Thanks." He grabs a brown sack lunch from his desk and finds his way outside.

I watch him from my own desk, enjoying the fact that he won't be able to see me staring. He tilts his face to the sun, sandwich abandoned on the bench beside him. Watching him, I feel almost like I can feel the sun's warmth on my own cheeks.

I close my eyes, soaking up the imagined sun.

When I open them, Sal is standing in front of my desk—belt, groin, and gun all front and center. I snap to attention. "Hey."

"What's up, Macie?"

Just staring at another guy. "Oh, thinking about this case."

"Getting sucked in, are you? Happens to us all." He smiles. It's a nice smile, really it is. He plops into the seat next to me. "Doing anything this weekend?"

Of course not is the actual answer. "Don't think so," I say. "Let me check."

I fumble with my phone as he says, "We could go to that Mexican place. And after that, I was thinking drinks or something. There's a new sports bar downtown."

I'm not super keen on sports or beer, but I nod, gazing at the blank weekend spaces on my phone.

"What day you thinking?" I ask.

"Friday good?"

I nod, like I can just barely squeeze him in. The fact that I don't really want to go doesn't fully register in my brain. A hot guy just asked me out. For a second date.

And so it's done. Dinner. Drinks. Sports bar. Friday. I'll meet him there and I'm kind of relieved he won't be picking me up.

When he stands I see that Tad has turned my direction, the blank stare. It occurs to me that, even from the courtyard where he's eating, he probably heard. Those perfect ears.

Turning away, I jam a cookie from my own lunch in my mouth, like a child trying to hide a lie.

CHAPTER 12

The first relative's house is an unholy kind of huge. Brick and stone and vaulted ceilings. Shrubbery in designs. Chandeliers. Fat rugs over dark, shiny hardwood floors. And—I'm not even kidding—they have a full-on set of armor in the front hall.

"You have a lovely house," I say with what I hope is a winning smile.

The man scowls back and gestures grudgingly to a sitting room. For real—a sitting room, like it's 1864 or something.

Tad is subtly sniffing, quietly tapping. He left his cane in the car and will occasionally touch my arm to check his bearings.

An actual maid brings out an actual coffee service

and I realize I'm wearing jeans and an ET t-shirt that I don't remember buying. Tad, as always, looks like he belongs on GQ, so he's fine. Even Anderson looks okay in his police blues.

"So?" the man says, sitting down in a smoking chair (yup, I said it, a smoking chair). He's wearing a designer shirt that fits perfectly over an excessively muscled chest and arms. Like, the dude's huge. Over six feet, maybe 300 pounds. All muscle muscle muscle. And did I mention muscle. Everywhere. Even the lines along his jaw ripple with strength when he moves his mouth. Not only is he a non-green version of the incredible hulk, but he's got gorgeous white teeth, a full head of nearly black hair, and the greenest eyes I've ever seen. But he still hasn't smiled.

"My condolences, Mr. Cane," Anderson begins. "On the death of your cousin, Phillip." The man snorts "Second cousin."

Anderson clears his throat.

"And no one called him Phillip. He was Phil, just Phil." A look creases his tan face and I lean toward that look. Sadness? Hard, deep sadness. It's gone in a moment. "Neither of them killed the other like you guys think. Phil didn't even like guns."

"He was in the military at one point," Anderson says. "And owned a gun."

"Who doesn't these days? I've got a whole collection," the man—Mr. Cane—says. I realize that Anderson didn't brief us on his full name, and I didn't ask. Tad's right—we're definitely not detectives.

Mr. Cane throws a hand toward an oak cabinet. "Can't use a one of them. Just like to look."

"Mr. Cane," Anderson says. "We're trying to understand what *did* happen to your cousin and his wife. Right now we don't have much to go on. Literally everything points to a murder-suicide."

"*Literally?*" Mr. Cane asks. "Then why are you here?"

Anderson pinches his lips closed and I catch myself kind of liking this Cane guy.

"We can't find a motivation," Anderson says lamely.

"No," Cane says. "You can't. And you won't. He didn't kill her."

"Then who might have?' Anderson asks.

Tad is leaning, and tapping. His mouth opens just a bit, and I swear he's tasting the air.

"No one. He was the nicest guy anyone ever met. His wife was a doll, too. She taught yoga at my gym in town."

Suddenly the name clicks. The muscles, the tan, the money, even the knight in the front hall. Arthur

Cane. This guy owns King Arthur's Gym and Day Spa. They have them all over the southern part of the state—upscale gyms that cater to the south's elite.

"Do you know where their dog is?" Tad asks. It's the first thing he's said.

Cane squints at him. "I assumed he was killed too. That animal would have fought to the death for them."

"If he did, we haven't found him," Anderson responds. "No sign of a dog's remains at all. The Samuelsons didn't ask you or any other relatives to keep him?"

"Not that I know of," Cane answers. "Of course, they wouldn't ask me. I have a horrible allergy."

"And you live alone?" Anderson asks.

Cane clears his throat and I remember some scandal. "My wife is not here at the moment," he says.

Tad tips up his chin. "Thank you for your time, Mr. Cane."

Anderson is rooted to the seat, glaring. I realize I haven't touched my coffee and take a quick slurp. Turns out rich people coffee tastes about the same, though they probably don't think so.

"I wasn't done," Anderson says after we leave. "This is NOT your investigation."

"You could have stayed," Tad says. "*I* didn't need to."

"So…?" Anderson says.

"Not him."

"And why not?"

"He's obviously sad. You could hear it in every inch of his voice."

"I couldn't," Anderson says.

"I know," Tad responds. "And there's not a hint of dog scent anywhere in the house. He wasn't lying about the allergy. But even more importantly—"

"—he's loaded like a potato," I finish.

Tad clicks his tongue. "Yup. No motivation."

"What about the dead wife?" Anderson asks. "Maybe she and Cane had a thing. She taught yoga at his studio. He and his own wife are clearly not living in the same wing of the house."

"There *was* a scandal of some sort," I say. "I can't remember the details."

"The details," Tad says, "was *women.* Plural. Not one, not a singular that he would kill or kill for, not one he would murder along with a relative he cared about, not one he'd risk in exchange for this whole precious lifestyle."

"Some guys can never get enough," Anderson says. "Girls, money, everything. Nothing stops them —they always want more."

For a strange moment the three of us pause in a bond of understanding. Yeah, *those* guys—the ones who have it all when we're just trying to scrape by. The cop. The lonely girl. The blind guy. Then the moment breaks.

"Not him," Tad says.

"Why not?" Anderson asks. "Maybe he thought he'd get some booty and an inheritance and got mad when he wound up with neither. Maybe he's in over his head and can't pay his bills—wouldn't be the first time a guy living like this was really on the brink of financial disaster."

"Maybe," Tad says, "But that's a fact you can check."

"And I will," Anderson says.

"I already did," Tad answers. "His gyms are doing great. They're adding another branch here soon. And the franchise is about to go national."

Anderson grunts, making a scribble in his notebook anyway.

"You sure the dog hadn't been there?" he asks, but even I can tell he's grasping now.

"Not a drop of dog scent," Tad continues.

"You can pay people to clean for that."

Tad looks skeptical about whether anyone could clean well enough to erase dog scent from his nose. "At any rate, it's clear that he doesn't need money, doesn't need one woman. In fact, he seems to struggle with the concept of monogamy. And he liked his cousin. I could tell. Macie could too."

Anderson turns to me, raises his eyebrow.

"Tell him about his hands, Mace," Tad says. "Did they fidget? Tremble? Give anything away?"

I get stuck for a second on the nickname Tad just gave me. *Mace.* I like it.

Anderson glares.

"No trembling," I say quickly, trying to remember the hands, to think of them as I would if I drew them. "One wedding ring. One college ring. Beautiful nails—no biting or any nervous habits; plus he has them done. They were polished like they do at salons. The backs of his hands were tan, and hairless—also probably done, considering his facial and chest hair." I blush and am relieved Tad can't see it.

Anderson rolls his eyes.

"So, yeah," I stumble, trying to sound as professional as Tad. "Nothing in his hands to indicate guilt."

"Well, thank heavens," Anderson says. "We wouldn't want him to have guilty-looking hands."

"But mostly," I continue. "He looked sad. But also

like he was trying to *not* look sad. The sadness would pop out every once in a while in the lines of his face. The sound of his voice. And it seems like if he was trying to fake not murdering someone, it would have looked the opposite—super sad with not-sad leaking through."

Anderson's shoulders slump like he's been beaten at a game he usually wins. I feel a little sorry for him till he says, "That's one down then. You calling an Uber, Simmons?"

"Macie's taking me."

"Of course she is." A quirk of his lips like he was laughing at me. I'd seen that look from my ex before; other people too. People who thought the things I did didn't matter much. "Enjoy the taxi job, Greene."

Tad's cheek quivers. I want to say something in Tad's defense, or maybe my defense—it's a little muddled in my mind—but realize that anything I say will either embarrass me or emasculate Tad.

"Next relative—a first cousin once removed—couldn't meet daytime either," Anderson says. "Turns out working people only come home at night."

"Turns out lonely guys don't," Tad retorts.

Anderson gets into his car and slams the door.

Tad's frowning. "Come on, Greene. Time to taxi me home."

"It's not a taxi," I say, wondering why he's suddenly using my last name, just like Anderson did. I almost add, *It's what friends do,* but the way Tad is scowling kills the words before they cross my lips.

CHAPTER 13

When I get home after eight, the meal delivery package is on my porch. I'd been planning on ordering takeout and bingeing Netflix.

But the bright green compostable box glares at me. "Alright, alright," I say, scooping it up like a lost cat, not a box of pre-chopped and measured food.

One thing about my ex, Alex—he could cook. Gorgeous, organic dishes. Why else do you fall in love with a man who is going to wander away? He could turn wilty spinach and a box of abandoned mushrooms into heaven on a plate.

"Just a little salt and butter," he'd say. In fact, he said it so often that I once had an apron made with those words embroidered on it—the only thing I gave him that he took when he left. Maybe the only time I understood or at least appreciated him.

When I made things with a little salt or butter they came out greasy or, well, salty. When he did, they came out reborn.

Unfortunately for me, he spoiled me without actually managing to teach me anything. Or maybe I just didn't manage to learn. Either way, I could never return to freezer dinners after our marriage, but I still wasn't great at putting butter and salt together in redemptive combinations, or even mildly satiable ones. And I didn't like to shop. Which left me with limited choices. The expensive green box it was.

Two chicken breasts, two garlic cloves, a bag of chopped celery and carrots, everything marching out in pairs like we were headed to Noah's ark.

I pull out Alex's frying pan, and yes, I still think of it as his, though it—like me—has been abandoned. The diced chicken goes into olive oil with a packet of just the right amount of seasonings—no salty, greasy soup for me tonight. Add the vegetables, water, bouillon, and then top it off with a dash of packaged creamer. Soup. It's not quite Alex's, but it's better than mine would have been and it's more comforting than the takeout I was going to get.

By the way, if you ever try to order one of these

green box meals for one, well, you can't. They come for two, or four. Something about shipping being worth it. Whatever. I eat leftovers. I guess it's what lonely people do. The thought reminds me of Tad's jab at Anderson.

Oh shoot. I stop mid-spoonful in the eating of my soup. I'm supposed to be on a date tomorrow night—the night we're meeting the next cousin. I leave a crust of French bread to soak in my soup and text Sal. "Something came up with work. Can't make it at six."

"No worries," he texts back almost immediately. "We'll skip the restaurant and just hit the bar. How about nine?"

It feels like a much drunker time of night, but I'd be a jerk to cancel completely when I know that the investigation won't last that late into the night. And I know Sal knows it too.

"Perfect," I reply, pausing at the blue send button, finger hovering. How will Tad get home? I mean, I can still drive him, of course, but if I didn't have plans, maybe I could linger and talk.

My finger stabs 'send.' What am I even thinking? We didn't linger tonight. We didn't talk, not even about the case. In fact, I drove him home and he barely said a word the whole time. He just scowled at nothing. Then jumped out of the car like he couldn't get away fast enough. For all I know, he'll just call an Uber next time anyway.

I tell myself it's because it embarrasses him—having to get a ride home. But I know that if he'd had even a millimeter of interest, he would have gotten over that, and maybe said a couple words.

I swab up the last few drops of my soup, thinking of his back, straight, broad, practically barreling toward his house. His house. It was a simple gray vinyl, rectangular, flat. No steps to navigate. Two shrubs on either side of his door, but no flowers, no shutters or winsome curtains. The door, however, had been cherry red with an oblong window at its center. One pretty bright spot in an otherwise blank slate. I smile thinking of it, then realize with some guilt that maybe that's how Tad is forced to see the world. Winsome curtains need not apply.

CHAPTER 14

Cousin number two is a redhead. She is *not* allergic to dogs and owns no less than five. As we walk in, four stand like sentinels at attention—full-sized poodles, two on either side of the hallway. A smaller one scrambles around at her ankles, not barking, though it clearly wants to. She sweeps it into her arms and settles it against her bosom (it's definitely a bosom), then waves toward a creamy white couch that hovers like a cloud over a dark mahogany floor. When you look at this place, you do not think 'dog owner.' There isn't a hair, scratch, or chew toy in sight. And those dogs by the door, they don't move an inch until she gives two distinct clicks with her tongue. At which point, they wander—or do they march; it's unclear—to the space around her armchair and settle in. I'm reminded of cheetahs resting at the foot of their queen.

Do I need to mention that cousin number two is also loaded? I legit feel like I stepped into the house of Queen Elizabeth or someone. I'm still waiting on tea when Anderson finally clears his throat and says with a tone of reverence, "You're the poodle whisperer. My wife saw you on YouTube. Now she follows your channel."

The woman, whose name has completely fled my low-society mind, nods slightly with a smile I imagine she would give to her favorite peasants. "My channel has become quite popular in recent years, Mr. Anderson."

Quite, I think. The house is draped fully in white from curtain to cupboard to chair. If St. Peter had come down the stairs to tell me I'd made it to the pearly gates, I'd have had no trouble believing it in these surroundings.

"Are you a dog lover, Mr. Anderson?" she asks. When she does I'm pulled away from the celestial décor long enough to notice two things: she doesn't call him 'officer' and she knows his name. Too bad I still don't know hers.

The file is on Tad's lap and I don't know how to reach over and grab it without making a spectacle of it.

"We've got a little goldendoodle ourselves," Anderson is saying.

"Lovely breed," she replies. "And quite popular right now."

Something in that tone says to me that she's unimpressed by popular things, but Tad and I aren't exactly jumping in to help with the small talk. Frankly, I'm still waiting for the tea and crumpets. Bonus points if it comes to me balanced on the head of one of those dogs, who have better posture than any human I've met, for the record.

None of them, however, seem interested in my refreshment. And, while I can totally imagine this woman and her terrifyingly well-groomed animals committing homicide, I can't imagine her doing it for money.

She's currently regaling Anderson with several tales (tails! Ha!) and tips for getting his Goldie to drink without slurping all over the floor. She manages to drop several celebrity names as she does so.

The dogs, and Anderson, hang on every word the woman speaks, though I notice that she occasionally glances toward Tad and it's a glance I recognize. Sizing him up—the posture, the fitted shirt, the beautiful waves of hair. She's trying to crack in.

Good luck, lady—I still can't figure out how to get the file off his lap.

But then, he looks at her—a straight-on gaze. I've never seen him do that before, didn't know he could. And I admit that in a weird way, I feel jealous.

"Ms. Houston,"—ah, that's the name; Regina Houston—"You've clearly got a gift. Did Phil and Melanie Samuelson ask you to watch their dog for a period of time?"

Everyone freezes for a moment, remembering why we're here.

"No," she hums, after the pause. "Bernard was always sent to another caregiver when they were away." She stops, strokes the lapdog like an evil genius would. "Not that they were away."

"Bernard?" I squawk, like I just stepped off the cast of the *Beverly Hillbillies*. Before she can answer, I suddenly realize she must be talking about the dog.

"Were they planning to go away?" Tad asks, not skipping a beat, though I get the impression that she intended to create a beat.

"Not that I'm aware of," she coos. "Of course it wouldn't have been my business if they did."

They weren't close.

"You weren't close," Tad says, like he just read my mind.

"Not particularly," she answers. The dogs gaze at her when she speaks. "Phil was much younger—his mother and I were cousins. And he was still a kid when I was making my way in this world. We were never doing the same sorts of things at the same time."

"Do you have the name of the person who is the dog's caregiver?" Anderson asks. "The dog is missing and we're trying to find it."

"Him," Regina Houston replies.

"Excuse me?" Anderson says.

"Bernard was a male," she says.

"You liked him?" Tad asks. "Bernard."

"I did," she answers.

"Did you help train him?"

"Phil called for a few pointers when Bernard was a puppy. I helped as much as I could. And Bernard seemed to learn well." She looks directly at Tad, like she's decided he's the one in charge of this investigation. "I didn't dislike my cousin. I just didn't know him well. We visited occasionally at holiday gatherings, funerals, Cane's recommitment ceremony just a month ago."

I quirk an eyebrow, though she doesn't notice.

"And I do know the caregiver's name, to answer your earlier question. I recommended him." She sets the small dog down and pulls open a drawer, retrieving her phone.

"But Bernard isn't with him. I called first thing when I heard the news. Would you like the number?"

"You called about the dog?" I ask, trying to keep my voice even.

"Yes, I called about the dog," she says, settling the blue ice of her gaze on me. I see instantly why her dogs obey. "I already knew about the people."

"We're so sorry for your loss," Anderson says.

With a slight tremble in her voice, she asks, "Do you think there's any chance Bernard might be alive?"

It's more emotion than she's shown the whole time. I don't know if I should be touched or disgusted.

"We haven't found it, um, him, dead," Anderson replies.

She regains her composure, puts the phone away. "Please let me know if that changes."

"Of course," Anderson says.

Tad tips his head to the side, not tapping, but listening.

I haven't done as well, hearing the words, the voice, but not the things that sometimes ride underneath or hum on top of them.

"It's clearly not her," Anderson says when we reach the street.

I'm inclined to agree, but uninclined to be agreeable. "That psychopath," I reply.

"She's a dog lover," he replies. "Publicly. Privately. That's not psycho."

I know he's clutching the business card she gave him in his pocket.

"She cared about the dog way more than the people. Maybe she killed them to get her precious Bernard, and then he ran away."

Tad laughs. "Come on, Macie."

I don't reply.

"You know she could have had Bernard if she'd wanted him."

"And why is that?" I ask.

He stares out over the dark evening. "Because her dogs bred him."

I stand there stupidly for a moment, knowing Anderson is smirking. Now that Tad's said it, it's too obvious. But I'm not ready to wave my truce flag. "How do you know?"

"How do you not?" Tad counters in a know-it-all voice that drives me nuts.

I take a breath, hear the memory of her voice, know I won't forget it. Soft, controlling.

"One of the other dogs also had a 'B' name," Tad says. "Beatrice. She called it into the room."

I shake my head. I can hear her voice perfectly, would recognize it over the phone or in any crowd, but I can't recall anything she said to the dogs.

"And each time she talked about Bernard, she leaned in toward that dog, Beatrice."

"How did you even *see* that?" I ask in a way that must be tacky and insensitive, but I don't care.

"I heard it," he says. "The movement. But even if I hadn't, she was wearing bright orange."

Anderson looks between the two of us, still smirking. "Besides," he adds. "She was also loaded. Like a potato, as Macie would say." He laughs, unlocking his cop car. "Last lead is in the daytime. Because the next guy—the nephew—he's an artist. That's more promising. Probably poor and lazy. Some millennial who's indignant he didn't get a piece of Granny's pie."

"How great," I say in a fairly impressive deadpan.

"This is on you two. If it were up to me the case would already be closed. Murder-suicide."

"But it isn't a murder-suicide," Tad says. "You know it too."

"Do I?" Anderson asks, getting into his car.

He does. I hear it just like Tad would, in the tones

of his voice. Not only that, but Anderson's enjoying it—this hunt. He's glad we sent him on it.

He pops open the door of the cop car and swings in, like he's the lone ranger, not some middle-aged policeman. "See you geniuses on Monday."

When he's gone, Tad asks, without turning, "You really didn't think it was her, did you?"

"So what if I did?"

"But you didn't," he says.

I look sideways at him, notice the profile—sharp jaw, soft cheeks. "No," I say. "Though I couldn't have said why like you did. Even though she is."

"Is what?" he asks.

"A psychopath. Who's loaded like a potato."

"Well, we've got the starving artist to look forward to."

"Goody." I glance at my watch. "Need a ride?"

"Nah, I've got an Uber coming."

I knew it.

"And you've got a date," he says.

I narrow my eyes at the sharpened silhouette that is his face. "How did you know?"

He laughs. "I hear things, remember? And I mean, it's not a secret, right?"

I shrug, though he probably can't see it. I want it to be a secret. And why, why do I want that?

"Have fun," he says. "You look nice."

"Do you even know what I look like?" I ask. "And I'm changing anyway."

"You're wearing blue," he says. "And it suits you."

As he says it, the Uber pulls up and he climbs in. "See you Monday, Mace."

I hold up my hand in good-bye, but forget to add words to it so he can hear. We're back to Mace now that he has a different ride and I'm going on a date with a different guy. If that's not the safety of the friendzone, I don't know what is.

CHAPTER 15

My date does go well, thank you very much.

I don't wear blue and opt instead for a fire engine red. Not a miniskirt or anything. I'm not insane. But I dig out a cute tank, some skinny jeans that suck me up in the right places and make things look smooth that are definitely not smooth.

Sal has already had at least a few drinks by the time I arrive, and I'm relieved. When guys are already a little loose, they don't notice as much when you're not. And I'm not.

I order—I'm not kidding—a virgin piña colada. The truth is that I'm not in the mood for a hangover, headache, or worse. And I have no desire to wake up in this guy's bed. Although, looking around, I can tell there are several girls at the bar who wouldn't mind.

The redhead two tables over keeps casting glances and then giggling to her friend. It makes me itchy because it feels like at least some of those giggles must be directed at me. *Why's a guy like that with a girl like her?* And, I mean, I see it.

Frumpy little me. Next to *him.* Sal's long brown fingers, the jet black hair, white teeth in his laughing face, plus he's probably pushing 6'5". Add to that the tight jeans, boots, and black cowboy hat. Why don't I want to wind up in his bed?

"Hey, Macie, let's dance," Sal says, grabbing my hand and leading me out to do some country line dance. Okay, maybe I should have had a *little* bit of rum in that piña. I'm all left feet. But—like I said—drunk guys don't notice. "You're good," he says, after we've knocked out the Cotton-eyed Joe and topped it with a sloppy Macarena. Now the music's slowed and he wraps me up into a slow sway. He smells like beer and pizza and laughter. And I realize that I don't want to wind up in his bed because I don't belong there. I'm too practical, wound up too tight.

He pushes his hips into mine, tucks his chin onto my head. It's sweet, and I feel the eyes of the redhead on us, other women too, even the bartender is staring. I let my head rest against his chest, try to give the music a chance to cast a spell on me.

It's warm; it's safe; it's sweet. He likes me as me. What else was it that I wanted?

The evening ends with a sloppy kiss in the parking lot by my car. I do my best to lean into it, though at the end I can't seem to resist talking. "I had fun," I say.

"You're beautiful," he gushes.

And he's drunk. I blush anyway. "Thanks, I..." Now I'm stuck.

He takes a slight step back and stumbles.

"We probably better call you an Uber." Yup, that's how I end the romantic exchange. Go me.

He glances at my car, and I bite back the invitation. *Or I could let you crash at my house.* It would definitely not land the way I want it to land.

"Yeah, shoot, guess I had too much."

"It happens," I say, adjusting the cowboy hat that has tipped to the side. I feel like an actor as I do it—a girl in a role, and something about that reminds me uncomfortably of my failed marriage.

"Next time," he says, winking. I blush again, pulling out my phone for the Uber.

He steals one more kiss just before the car arrives and I let him, but I have to admit that I'm mildly relieved to see him go. And then I have to admit that something is definitely wrong with me. His t-shirt stretches across the tight muscles of his back as he climbs in and his smile is as bright as the lamp overhead.

"You're crazy," a voice behind me says as he drives off. I turn to see the redhead, her friend nowhere in sight.

"I know," I say, squinting up at the street lamp.

"Just let a butt like that climb in and drive away."

I nod. "I was married before," I say. "It hurt."

She laughs. "I'm not saying you had to marry the dude." She slips off the white heels, hooking them onto her fingers as she waits for her ride. "You sure you don't swing another way?"

It's meant as an insult. But the truth is that I'm really not sure what's wrong with me. Marriage or no, shouldn't I be interested at least, even if it's something shallow? But then I see Tad's fingers, tapping along the fabric of somebody's couch, desk, papers, and my heart scatters. "Naw," I say to the girl as her ride pulls up. "Thanks for the offer, though."

I enjoy the catch of surprise on her face as her friend pops the door open. "See you around," I say. I don't have to be completely basic, after all.

CHAPTER 16

See, the thing was, when I said *See you around,* it was supposed to be one of those snarky, cool kid things. Not literal. Not like there she is sitting at the receptionist's desk, same white heels, our new temp. She's replaced the hot popular one who, rumor has it, got a permanent job at a doctor's office in town.

So now the redhead's sitting there at the receptionist's desk. The *new* new girl.

"Crap," I say, staring.

Even though I'm the only one muttering under my breath, I'm not the only one staring. The whole highly testosterone-infused office is whirring in her direction.

"What?" Tad asks from his desk beside me. He's got his nose up to some paperwork he's reading.

"Nothing," I grumble.

"New girl got you down?" he asks, not moving his nose from the paper. "Another act in town."

"Another *act*?" I say. "That's more than a little sexist. We are not 'acts' in town." Tad doesn't answer, not even to shrug.

"I'm not an act," I grumble and he tips his shoulders in my direction.

"Look at this," he says just as Richards saunters over to the new girl. Sal's eyes follow.

Tad taps the paper down, stabbing at the center. "Cane's involved in another scandal. This one a domestic. He pulled a gun."

"Really?" I say, genuinely interested. "He said it was just a collection."

"Who collects guns and doesn't use them?"

No one in Kentucky, that's for sure. But I'm still surprised.

"Guess his wife came home tipsy and he thought she'd been with another guy," Tad continues. "Set him off."

We both hear laughter from the front desk. He tilts his head that direction. "What's she look like?"

I shake my head. "Red hair."

"Natural?" he interrupts.

"Yeah," I say. "And curled—not natural. Blue eyes,

big lips and butt. She's pretty," I say. "You should ask her out."

"Nah," he responds, picking the report up from my desk and cramming it to his face. "I'm not into standing in lines. Besides, beauty is wasted on the blind."

"Your loss," I reply. "I'm sure those hands make a good enough set of eyes."

"Macie!" he says, kind of laughing though. Then, "Who's sexist now?"

"Just fact-ist. Men like something soft to grab."

"That the problem with your ex, then?" Tad says, paper still to his nose, though he'd gotten to the bottom of the document, the top flopping over as he focused on the last few lines. "Too grabby and needy?"

Hardly. On either point. Too head in the clouds, Mount Everest level. Barely noticed me, definitely didn't need me, except to pay the bills I guess. "No," I say. "He was perfectly independent." Well, except in adulting.

"Ah," Tad says, finally setting the report down. "Perfectly, huh?"

Time to change the topic. I take a jab at the report. "Cane might have a temper problem, but he's still loaded like a potato, and he still cared about Phillip. Still without a motivation."

"True," Tad says, "and he didn't hurt a fly, just swung a gun around. Never even fired. Charges were dropped a few hours later."

"Of course they were." All the unhappy couples, hating each other nearly to death, but staying together. At least Alex had given me that much dignity—to leave when things were finished.

"You haven't moved for over a minute," Tad says. "You're staring."

"You're one to talk," I shoot back without thinking about what I'm saying, and then realize I'm probably the worst person ever.

Tad doesn't seem to care though. "Ouch," he replies just as Sal plants himself firmly in front of my desk.

"Had a great time Friday, Macie. We should do it again." He turns to Tad. "Did you know this girl could dance?"

"I had no idea," Tad answers.

My face is hot, my neck probably purple.

"How about this weekend?" Sal asks.

"Sure," I say, "but Tad and I have work to do on this case right now…"

"Sure, sure," he says, backing away with a wink and a flash of white teeth.

"Sounds like things are going well," Tad says.

"I can't dance," I mutter back. "Sal was just drunk."

"So, they didn't go well?" he asks.

I lift a shoulder, a shrug probably too subtle for him to see.

"Things are just…" I begin, "…going."

"I see," Tad says.

And the thing is, maybe he does.

CHAPTER 17

We drive in Anderson's cop car, past the dilapidated houses at the south end of downtown. The roof on one has caved, while the house right next door is leaning onto it. Together, they look like a couple of drunk frat boys at a party.

"They did a meth bust there last week," Anderson is saying. He's chronicled several recent crimes on our trip to the inner-city address and we're all gearing up to meet the starving-artist-murder-for-money nephew, when the neighborhood turns.

Suddenly, the houses are standing up straight. Then we notice new paint, wrap around porches that haven't collapsed, windows with bright lights shining through them.

I can't swear to it, but I'm pretty sure the side of Tad's mouth quirks up. He's staring out the window even though I know it's just a blur of color to him, when Anderson says, "Well, that's interesting." The pavement smooths. Flowers start to appear in pots and then the pots get bigger or sometimes become entire trellises with blooms that cascade down the walls of newly renovated Victorian houses.

"Ah, the art district," Tad says. "Always full of surprises."

"I knew they'd been doing work here," Anderson says. "But wow."

At this point, the houses are more than renovated. Floor-to-ceiling windows twinkle inside with soft light. Gardeners dot the wrought-iron encased lawns. We rumble off the pavement and onto the 200-year-old cobblestone of the historic district. Anderson checks his GPS.

"I don't suppose anyone googled this guy?" I ask.

From Anderson's curse, I'm guessing it's a 'no,' which seems a little ridiculous with him being a detective and all, but I don't mention that part. From Tad's smirk, I'd have to say that he's a 'yes.'

In one more decadent block, our starving artist morphs into a nationally-acclaimed painter.

"He just did a show at the MOMO," Tad says,

holding up his phone. "A display where he sat with a collection of antique vacuum cleaners and didn't move for twelve hours and wore a Depends diaper just in case."

"Gross," I say.

"Rich," Anderson adds.

"Loaded," Tad quips.

"Like a potato," I finish, trying not to giggle.

Anderson doesn't even crack a smile.

And, I mean, maybe the nephew murdered his aunt and uncle and stole their dog. Maybe he stuffed Bernard into an antique vacuum so he could stare at it all day, but walking up the concrete steps that glitter with bits of sea glass and shell and flakes of upcycled metal that have been set into them, it's clear that the nephew's only motivation could be insanity—money having been taken completely out of the equation.

Tad tip taps on the door anyway, the smile of a mad genius on his face, in counterpoint to Anderson's scowl. Seeing it, I realize Tad's been planning this—some sort of retribution for the two evening appointments.

And I'm not even kidding—a servant answers the door. Some dude dressed up like a butler only...sexier.

We're led through a hall filled with images of the nephew's art intermingled with framed photographs of naked body parts from people of all genders. He seems to have an affinity for tattoos as well.

Tad has the good fortune of missing the barrage of nudity and Anderson is full-on squirming. Me too, if I'm honest.

Our host greets us in a bathrobe slightly open at the top so that his chest bush can be appreciated in all its curly bronze glory.

"Oh dear," he says. "I do love a man in uniform."

Anderson's about to lose it, and I can't help but feel a little bad for him.

"Sorry," I interrupt, "he's married."

"Pity," says the nephew, whose name is Chad Porterhouse. "But those things can change. Take my card, darling." He shoves a bright triangular business card in Anderson's direction.

"Actually, Mr. Porterhouse," Anderson says, collecting himself and waving the card away. "We're here—as you know—to discuss the case concerning Mr. and Mrs. Samuelson."

I snatch the card before Porterhouse can put it back in his robe or chest hairs or wherever he was hiding it. He raises an eyebrow at me, and then winks. "Keep it, Queen. And call me if you need…something."

"Mr. Porterhouse," Anderson says. "Can we please stay with the case?"

Waving a hand in the direction of a different room, Porterhouse says, "Ugh. Dreadful stuff. How awful of you to bring it up."

Anderson sighs and Tad rocks back on his heels, enjoying the show. We're seated in a variety of colorful chairs, none of which is particularly comfortable. I sink into mine so deeply I know there's not going to be a ladylike way to extricate myself, and Tad's has a headrest thing that pokes him in the back.

"It is dreadful," Anderson says, turning his chair to the side to get the most comfortable angle for his bottom. "Thus this visit." The scantily clad butler brings us lemon waters and martinis. I almost expect Anderson to throw his back, but he sticks to business.

"Can't believe he did it," Porterhouse goes on. "Uncle Phil put up a good front."

"Front?" Anderson asks.

"Of course. The cute suburban house, the department store dinnerware, the family dog, even the fertility issues. So wonderfully cliché."

Tad tilts his head to the side on the word 'fertility.' It's something no one else has mentioned, but instead of steady-headed policing, I find my gut sinking as I remember Rachel and Aiden—those years of trying, then their sweet little Gabby—like a star dropped in their laps. And then, Rachel gone. Just like that.

"Mr. Samuelson didn't kill his wife," I interrupt, and Anderson stares daggers at me.

"Oh, didn't he?" Porterhouse asks.

"Ms. Greene misspoke," Anderson says with a sharp click on the 'k' sound. "But yes, the case *is* under investigation."

"Oooohhhh, how exciting!" Porterhouse says.

"You mean 'tragic,'" I reply.

"I mean," he replies, not backing down. "Out of the ordinary."

"That it is," Tad intervenes. "Did your uncle indicate where they might have been boarding their dog?"

"My uncle," Porterhouse replies, "did not *indicate* anything to me. We weren't on speaking terms."

Anderson looks like he doesn't blame the uncle one bit.

"We rarely saw eye to eye." Porterhouse leans forward, then suddenly claps his hands. I jump.

"OMG. Does that make me a suspect?" he asks. "How delightful."

"Two people are dead," Anderson says. "It's not delightful. It's not fun."

"Two people and maybe their dog," Porterhouse replies.

"This is not a game," Anderson says.

"Unfortunately not," Porterhouse replies. "And unfortunately for you, I was in New York City at the time, a part of living art, so I cannot be implicated in this crime. This murder." He pauses grandly. "Or dognapping."

"Mr. Porterhouse," Tad says patiently. "We're not here to implicate you in anything."

I'm less sure of this by the second. I would personally love to implicate him in everything right now. Seems to me that Mr. Depends Diaper Living Art could murder just about anything except his own ego.

"We just want to know if you have information. The dog's whereabouts perhaps. Or anything else."

"Enemies?" the nephew asks, leaning forward eagerly.

"Sure," Tad replies indulgently.

"Nope," Porterhouse says flippantly rocking back and swigging down his martini. "No enemies at all. They just had dull friends in a dull life without baby or even nephew."

"You've mentioned that twice," Tad says. "The baby."

"They couldn't have a kid," Porterhouse says. "I'm

sure you know that. They'd been trying for years. I offered a sperm and you're not going to believe this, but they turned me down."

"Why do you hate them?" I ask abruptly.

Anderson throws up his hands and Porterhouse rolls his eyes. "Please," he says, waving me away. "Don't be such a simpleton."

I shrink at the word, at his gesture.

"I don't *hate* them," he says. "But they bore me. Uncle Phil wanted me to go to college, even offered to help pay. His sister—my mother—was in chemo at the time and not exactly rolling in cash. But I didn't want to go to college, refused actually. So I went to New York, worked on the streets."

I lift an eyebrow.

"Selling *art*," he says.

"Living art," I mutter under my breath, but he doesn't hear.

"Anyway, I swear my uncle still blames me for Mom's death. The stress and worry and blah blah blah. But I loved her too. And she had cancer. Think whatever you will about me—most of it is probably true—but I dedicated my first show to her."

I hope it wasn't vacuums.

"*And* donated all the proceeds to the Josephine Cancer Institute where she was treated. And, frankly, there were a LOT of proceeds."

"No doubt," Tad says.

"As for the inheritance," Porterhouse says. "Since that's clearly why you're here. I obviously don't need it." He swings an arm around. "But as my mother's only heir, I did *deserve* half of it. Another slight from a family that had no room for minds that didn't fit into their own tight molds."

"Thank you for your time, Mr. Porterhouse," Anderson says.

"Time is all we've got," he replies.

And I want to punch him, really I do. If that's basic, then so be it.

"I'm sorry for your loss," Tad says. There's a gentleness to it that I can't understand. We turn to leave.

Porterhouse huffs. "The fertility doctor was called Matthews or something. Maybe he has some helpful information. After all, when you're trading sperm, things can get dicey."

"Thank you," Tad says, but I hate this guy even more. *Trading sperm.* Like he's ever wanted something he couldn't have. Like he could even understand that. On the way out, I let my allergies have full sway and sneeze on a watercolor featuring a photo of *living art*. It's in a glass frame and that sexy butler will surely hustle out and clean it, but it makes me feel a little bit better anyway.

ell, he didn't do it either," Tad says as we drive away.

"I wish he did," I say, slumping down in the seat. "How could he be so callous about their fertility?"

"Easy, Macie," Tad says.

"I'd love to see him locked up," I say. "Gray walls, basic square room, no hot butler."

"Hot, huh," Tad says.

"Honestly, Tad."

Anderson glances at us in the mirror. "That guy was a jerk, but he didn't kill them. Let's assess what we have."

I cross my arms.

Tad turns to me to try to see me. I angle away and look out the window.

"Fertility doc," Tad says.

"Doggie day care," Anderson adds, "even though the dog supposedly wasn't there. But we also know he's got a groomer and stuff. All that drama with Arthur Cane and his wife."

I stay silent, watching the houses shrink back into the slums. Drab colorless houses mushing together. Scruffy kids slipping through the lawns, dogs on chains. One barks. Something tip taps against my brain, something I can't quite place. Right now I don't even want to. I shove this stupid case aside. Today is Rachel's daughter's birthday, and I still haven't called.

CHAPTER 18

Rachel's daughter, Gabby, is already in bed when I call, but Aiden assures me she's still awake from the excitement of the day. *Me too, little sister. Me too.*

She tells me about her preschool teacher, Miss Mallow. "She has yellow hair," Gabby informs me. Yellow hair, just like Gabby, so different than her mother's thick, dark hair.

"You mean blond," I say.

"Okay," she answers, in the way young kids do when they're not quite listening anymore.

"What'd you eat for your birthday?" I ask.

That was the right question. "Pizza!" she says. "With cheese. Then choc'late cake with choc'late ice cream and choc'late sprinkles."

"No wonder you're not tired," I say, smiling on

my end. Who would want such a day to end?

"Daddy got me a bracelet-making kit and a red bow for Baby."

It takes me a second to remember that Baby is her stuffed giraffe.

"Wow. Baby got a gift too."

"Yes," Gabby says matter-of-factly, then yawns hard into the phone.

"Okay, pumpkin," I say. "Birthday wishes." I blow into the phone and she laughs then hands it back to Aiden.

"Sounds like life is good," I say when he's left Gabby's room.

"It's not bad," he replies. "Man, she grows fast. Birthdays just kill me."

"How's everything in the tech world?"

"Interesting to nerds as always. And you?" he says. "You're the one with the cool new job. Katie told me all the gossip."

She couldn't have told him everything since most of it is confidential and she's still out on leave.

"Well, I'll be happy when Kate's back at the receptionists desk," I say. "How's her new baby? Another boy, right?"

"They can't seem to make anything else," he replies. "But seriously, how's your job?" he repeats.

"You working with the police—that's something I didn't see coming."

"Me either." I say. "It's not quite the same as dentistry."

"Now you're the one with the exciting, dangerous job and I'm the one in an office," Aiden says.

"Don't know that I'd call it that exciting," I say.

"What would you call it then?" he asks.

Frustrating, I think, feeling the tip tap against my brain. The bark of a dog. Where is it? Who killed them? Why do I care? I'm just supposed to be there for observation—for my ears and eyes and photographic memory. "Aiden," I say a little abruptly, "when you used to fight fires and dogs were there, what would happen? Where would they go?"

"Animals are pretty resourceful," he says. "Often they find a broken window or opening to wriggle through and escape. And, of course, you've always got the stories of them dragging babies out or barking until we find them with their owners, though I've never experienced that myself. But I did once get a family out and then the dog came bounding out of this field toward them and it was sweet."

"Yeah," I murmur.

"And then, of course," Aiden continues. "Sometimes they just get trapped and die. It's really sad."

"Yeah," I say.

"Why do you ask?" he says.

I figure I can tell him since the dog isn't actually the case. "We've got a case and the dog is missing."

"People too?" he asks.

"Not exactly."

"Well," he replies. "If you can find the dog, my guess is you'll find someone connected to it."

<hr>

When I'm done, I text Tad. "Let's try the dog boarder."

"Glad you're done sulking and back in the game," he replies. "But a step behind. Anderson already called. The boarder hasn't seen the dog in months and has records to prove it."

"Shoot."

"Also, Anderson's getting a statement from the fertility doctor."

"We won't get to interview him?" I text.

"It's not TV—that's what Anderson said."

"Like we haven't just interviewed a bunch of people over the last few days." I hope Tad gets a sense of me grumbling through the text.

"The doctor's a professional, so they get a professional statement."

Yeah, because professional was the theme of those interviews.

"What about the groomer?" I ask. "The one from the recording."

"We don't even know which groomer it is," he texts back.

I purse my lips at every word in the text. I can practically hear him. *We're not detectives, Macie.* But more and more I feel like one. So if that makes me 'done sulking' then fine.

TAD

I'd never seen Macie lose her cool before. And it's not like she totally lost it—screaming or throwing punches. She just checked out.

I knew as soon as that stripper opened the door that Anderson would lose it, but I hadn't expected Macie to follow suit.

I reverse sequence the conversation in my brain, the scene coming to me backwards. And there's the moment. Fertility doctor. That's when he found his way under her skin. So she wanted a baby. Maybe that's even what led to her divorce. Apparently stuff like that is hard on couples. Not that I'd know.

It also explains why she's dating Sal. He seems like the hyper-fertile type. Otherwise, it was hard to imagine him as Macie's style—too forward, too frontal. But maybe that's where the appeal is. And even I have to admit that he's a nice guy. The kind of country boy who went to church on Sundays, helped Daddy with the farm, complimented old ladies, but with those olive features.

My jealousy spikes for a second. Some guys just seem to get all the luck—brawn, height, country kindness. But I bet Porterhouse would have thrown Sal off too. Just because you can flatter your mama's book club members doesn't mean you can get info out of a successful narcissist. But I did.

I hold my phone up to my good eye, reading, thinking. This fertility doctor is one of the best. People fly to Lexington from all over the country for an appointment with him. But Porterhouse is right. Trading sperm and making babies in a dish can get dicey, especially if the doctor has a perfect reputation on the line.

What if something went wrong?

What if they'd threatened to sue?

It could bring his empire down, even if he won.

Anderson would be pulling the medical records, but it would really be nice to talk to him. Nice, but not how things like this were done.

My Uber turns into the parking lot of a tall building—all windows and soft lighting. It looks like a spa for humans, not dogs.

"You forgot your pooch, man," the driver says

with a smile. His voice is young, thick southern accent.

I tip my head to the side, shifting my focus to him. "Just getting some estimates," I reply.

"Could have saved yourself some time and just asked me," the driver says, his accent dripping like a country song. "Estimate: My college tuition."

I laugh. He's probably not wrong.

"Spray your dog with a hose and towel it off. That's what my mama always did. It worked out."

"I bet it did," I say as a red sedan turns into the parking lot. I squint out the window. Was it? "But it turns out I'm really just meeting a friend."

The driver looks at the car. Macie gets out. "Hmm. Not bad looking, but a piece of advice from a fellow dude. Ditch her and find someone who doesn't need you to meet her at a dog salon."

"I'll consider your advice."

"Not mine," he says, as I open the door. "That little tidbit's from my mama. Nobody needs a girl just to take his money. No matter what else she gives, if you know what I'm saying."

"She's got plenty of her own money," I say.

"Doesn't mean she can't make a grab for yours too."

"That from your mama?" I ask, taking my cane from the seat beside me.

"Nope. That's my own bit of wisdom."

I tip him thirty percent. The kid's trying to make it through college, after all.

Macie has stopped to stare.

I walk cautiously to her, using my cane mostly to manage the curb. "Great minds," I say when she walks toward me.

"Or something like that," she grumbles.

"How'd you figure out which groomer it was?" I ask.

"I called a bunch," she says. "Till one sounded right."

It's impressive how well she can recognize voices, even with her sight.

"And you?" she asks.

"I looked up Anderson's record of recently paid bills."

She doesn't answer and I have to admit that I hate it when she does that. Maybe she shrugged or nodded, but if she did, I didn't catch it.

"So here we are," I say.

"My idea," she says finally. "You listened."

Now it's my turn not to respond. I did listen, but only because I'm not sure where else to look. And it feels like we should be looking *somewhere*.

"Anderson has this case all tied up and tucked

away," she says, looking around at the sleek stone walls.

"Does he?" I ask as she turns a circle. I squint to see what she's looking at. High ceilings, shelves lined with designer dog products. Most of it's a blurry smudge for me, because the thing I'm really bowled over by is the heavy scent of essential oils and doggie shampoos, the drone and buzz of clippers, the spray of water. Classical music pumps from the sound system, trying to distract me from it all, but it's not nearly enough to drown out the sound of dogs whining and barking, or to cover the smell of wet animals.

Macie holds a hand up to her face. "Have mercy," she grumbles. "I thought it'd be nice."

"It is," I say. "It's just…wet dogs."

She sniffles.

"Allergies?" I ask.

"They usually only bug me with dust or pollen. But… it's just a whole lot of fragrance."

A woman breezes through the door. She's a blur of pink lab coat and perfume. So much perfume. I can't tell if it's her own scent or one she uses on the dogs. Lavender and vanilla with a bit of musk underneath.

"How can I help you?" she asks.

"I," Macie begins.

"We," I insert, "were referred a month ago by some friends. We wanted to stop in and see the facility."

"Wonderful," she says, though I'm pretty sure Macie is scowling and trying to hide it. I can tell because her whole body always tenses up in this tight, tall line. "And who was it that referred you?"

"Well," I begin.

"Melanie Samuelson," Macie replies. My guess is that she's watching the woman's face, looking for a reaction. I do the same, only with my ears. I don't know what Macie sees, but all I hear is sadness.

"Oh," the groomer says. "I'm so, so sorry for your loss. That was just devastating."

"Bernard is still missing," Macie says, plowing ahead with her non-subtle method.

"Still?" the woman replies. "How awful. A detective actually called a few days ago to see if we'd boarded him, but that's not even something we do."

I nod, take a risk. "He was such a great dog."

"The sweetest," she says. "The whole family was. I just can't believe it."

Macie doesn't reply and from the other room, we hear a howl.

"Well, let me show you the facility," the pink woman says.

She's holding something, a clipboard I believe.

But she doesn't use it to write or anything, just holds it to her chest like a safety blanket.

We see the shampoo room, haircut room, even a massage room. I don't see as much as smell, hear. I want to stay in the dry massage room where no one is barking, but Macie pushes on.

"Did they mention they'd be boarding him somewhere?" Macie asks, trying to sound casual.

"Not at all?" the woman replies. "In fact, they were getting him all dolled up for something. A marriage or commitment ceremony or something."

"And where do you refer people—for daycare services?" I ask.

"We've got a couple places we trust. I take my own Peewee to this one. Love them." She thrusts a card into my hand.

"Thank you," I say. "You've been so helpful."

"I really am sorry about your friends. Life's too short, huh?"

We both nod solemnly.

"And what was your dog's name?" she asks. "So I can look for her if you bring her in."

"Princess," Macie answers just as I say, "Waldorf."

"Princess Waldorf," Macie finishes without skipping a beat. Then she leans in toward the woman, whispers, "Sometimes you have to compromise."

"Oh, I know. You wouldn't believe some of the hyphenated dog names we get in the shop."

I laugh inside. I *would* never have believed it if she hadn't said it.

A frazzled woman, soaked from wrist to shoulder, barrels into the room holding a large dog on a leash.

"Oh," she says, her voice falling when she sees us. "I thought it was the Williamses. They're late again."

The other woman clucks at her in a soothing tone. "Mrs. Williams struggles with that hip."

Macie is staring at the wet woman.

"Well, she could get her slow hip out the door a little sooner then," the wet woman replies.

The pink lab coat lady takes the leash from the woman. "Go take your break." There's a customers-are-here charge to her voice, but also a softness that I notice is always there. The dog settles as soon as she has the leash.

"Friends of the Samuelsons," she says delicately as the woman washes her hands.

The other woman leans. "Such a sad funeral."

"We were out of town," Macie says, her head tilting down, and I swear, I almost believe her.

"We miss Bernard," the wet woman says, fishing for something in her pockets and pulling out a silver flash—probably a lighter, or a Juul. "Jerry there could take a lesson." She bends toward the large dog.

The pink lady nudges her out the door and turns to us. Jerry's a perfect gentleman at her hand. "We hope to see Princess Waldorf soon," she coos.

"Of course," Macie coos back. I'm impressed. I've never heard her coo. I note the softness with just a bit of force in it.

"Well, they're nuts," she says when we get to her car. "But not dog murderers. Not even the lady with Jerry. Did you see that dog's goofy teeth?"

She stops abruptly, clears her throat.

"I did not," I say, smiling, though I'm not sure if she sees. "Do you think we smell like dog?"

"Probably just lavender."

"And vanilla," I mutter. "They were nice."

"Yeah, I'd bring my dog here. If I had one," she says.

"Would you?" I ask.

She laughs. "Actually, no. I could never afford it." She stuffs the brochure in my face and I hold it to my eye. My Uber guy was right.

"But would you want to," I ask. "If you could afford it?"

"Seems like a hose out back would work just fine."

I laugh. "If you weren't dating Sal, I'd have the perfect guy for you."

"We're not really dating," she mutters. And there are moments—maybe fewer than a person with regular sight might expect—but moments when I want to see, really see. Deep into someone's eyes, notice the flinches, the nervous glances. I fix my good eye on her face. She looks away, simple as that.

"So nothing—"

"—nothing that is any of your business," she finishes for me. And now the voice is all ice shards. I can read that easily enough. I wonder again about the way she lost it talking about the fertility doctor, wonder if she's disappointed about their non-dating status. And then I get the craziest idea.

"Listen," I say. "There's one more place we need to check out. One more place Anderson contacted, but I'd like to get a better sense of it."

I can't see her face well, but from the tight way she's holding her body, I get the idea she's narrowing her eyes.

"Where?" she says.

"I think you know."

She moves, shifting away from me. I can tell that she's moved her gaze too—off to the side, to the clouds, the sky, somewhere far away. I read once that the people do that—look to the horizon or other faraway objects when considering something lofty.

"I'll think about it," she says.

"I'll text you," I reply.

Maybe she nods. I can't tell. Her keys clink. I lean a little forward, hoping she'll offer me a ride. Like friends. She doesn't.

Finally, after a pause that even two non-hyper observant people would recognize as awkward, she asks, "Your Uber coming?"

"Yeah," I say, though I haven't called.

Macie leaves. She doesn't peel out, though it has that mood.

From a little table that sits at the side of the salon, I catch a glimpse of vapor. The wet woman must be there, still on her break. So she's seen. The happy fake couple leaving in different vehicles. It can't be the worst thing she's seen, not at a place like this.

I pull out my phone, tap it, and give the voice command for Uber. I'm hoping for the same guy. I'll tell him his advice was sound—that you can't trust a girl who goes to a dog salon.

CHAPTER 19

I leave thinking about Tad's idea. A fertility clinic. *The* fertility clinic. It's crazy. But he's right—it's the one place we haven't gone to check. Then I pause. No. Not the one place. There's another, maybe much simpler, place to check first.

I type 'humane society' into my GPS. Turns out, it's not even far away. And if you were a wayward dog, well, isn't that where you'd wind up?

I drive past the sign. It's so unassuming that I have to do a double back. Swallowsville Humane Society. It's a bland brick building tucked into a district mostly reserved for warehouses, but it's got a nice green patch of lawn and a big set of double doors.

I pull into the nearly empty parking lot and tap the steering wheel. Anderson said he'd check with the local rescues, but I know that means a couple phone calls at best, and suddenly I want to see for myself. I mean, maybe it was the owner of the shelter that killed them to get their hands on whatever type of poodle Bernard is. And then left him in a cage in the back room.

Okay, maybe my theory doesn't hold a *ton* of water, but I still want to see for myself, maybe ask a few questions.

A regular Nancy Drew right here.

Truth be told, I've never once in my life been to a humane society. That's not the kind of childhood I had. "Pets shed." That's what my mom said. Every time I'd ask if we could *just look.* When I walk into the building, it's clear that she wasn't wrong. Even so, the cages are neat and clean. I mean, I'm not sure what I was expecting—something depressing— caged animals staring at me with doleful eyes. And there's a little of that as I wander past the cats at the front, but the lights are cheery, the front lobby lined with chipper red chairs, and most of the animals are eating or sleeping or playing. Some of the cages are big—more like rooms with several kittens in them, and I see a sign pointing me to cat alley. No thanks, guys. I'm here on business.

Business that lingers in front of the cage of a little gray tabby—maybe four months old.

"You like silvers?" an older man asks from behind, and I swear at first I think he's referencing his own gray hair and hitting on me.

He nods to the kitten. "Silvers," he repeats.

"Oh, no," I stammer. "I was just glancing."

"You'd be surprised what can start from a glance," he says with a wink.

I'm *pretty* sure he's not hitting on me, though it's still a little unclear. But he's wearing a nametag. John.

"Would you like to take any of them out?" John asks, and I back up, waving my hand.

"Oh no, no, that's okay." And then my inner detective, or at least some version of common sense kicks in and I realize it looks weird to be at a shelter if you seem to be terrified of touching anything.

"Sometimes they trigger my allergies," I lie.

"Even the shorthairs?" he asks.

I clear my throat, realizing I don't really know how allergies and cats work. "Sometimes," I say. Yup, I'm basically James Bond.

"We've got a pretty little Siberian mix," he says. "They're good for allergy sufferers. But I think he's in cat alley. Which probably *isn't* good for your allergies. Or, how about this Oriental shorthair right here. An adult already, but barely."

Before I can think of a plausible excuse, the cat is in my arms, padding at my stomach.

"He's cute," I say.

"There's a play room right here." He unlocks a door with a small chair and a few cat toys. The little short hair pees as soon as I set him down. That doesn't bode well. I kind of stare at it, not knowing what to do. John notices and rushes to the rescue.

"There's a reason we do concrete décor around here."

I smile, come clean, sort of. "I'm really just here to look. Like, maybe at some dogs."

"Sure," he says, taking the cat and cradling it for a moment before returning him to the cage. "Just give me one minute." A pair of gloves, wad of paper towel, and few squirts of disinfectant later, and we're ready to go.

"You know we have a dog walking program every Saturday," he says as we make our way through a hallway to the back part of the shelter.

"That's a great idea."

"Yeah, gives them some much needed exercise and gives people a chance to get to know them."

I hear the dog section before I see it.

"If you're ever interested, I can sign you up." John

unlocks a door and when he does, he unleashes a decibel level of approximately ten trillion. I don't know what I was expecting from the dog zone, but after the quiet of the cat area, I'm unprepared for the barking, howling, echoing-off-the-concrete-walls room. I literally start to bring my hands up to cover my ears.

I catch myself and stop, but the sound is nearly unbearable. And dogs do doleful eyes better than cats. But they also jump up on the cage doors and bare their teeth occasionally.

"Any poodles?" I ask, feeling invisible amid the aural din.

He laughs. "Not even a mix. They're too popular these days. Plenty of pit blends, a few lab mixes, some little guys with unclear parentage."

"Yeah," I say, looking around. I'm trying to separate the barks into different sounds, the way I can do with human voices, but it's much more difficult. They all mesh together. I can pick out highs and lows, sharp or deep, but that's just about it. At his size, Bernard would probably be right in the middle—not shrill, not shake-your-bones-bass. A solid bark of a solid dog. I'd never find it in here.

"Oh," I say, not having to work too hard to feign disappointment. "I was definitely hoping for a poodle."

He laughs. "If you'd like I can add you to a waiting list and give you a call if we get one in."

"That might work," I say.

"And come on by Saturday for that walking program. Heck, you don't even have to wait; we're nearly closed; I could connect you with a dog to walk right now."

He's so nice and I feel like basically the biggest jerk of ever, but I have no desire to try to walk one of these dogs. I'm pretty sure they would wind up walking me. And what if one got away from me; what then?

"I'll have to think about it," I answer.

He shoves a dog walking form into my hand, and then I'm back in my car, headed to home. To utter silence. I look down at the form. Maybe I should fill it out and walk some dogs on a Saturday.

In the morning, I walk past the redheaded receptionist. For some reason, I want to catch her doing her nails or brushing her hair or something that seems frivolous. Instead, she's diligently doing her paperwork. Not only that, but she's dressed perfectly professionally—dark slacks, gray blouse, black ballet flats.

Better than me. I'm wearing a t-shirt with Yoda and jeans.

She catches me staring and smiles.

I look away, glancing toward Tad's desk—his head is down. I avoid glancing at Sal's desk.

Truth be told, I've been avoiding Sal all week. Any time I sense him heading to my desk, I head to the bathroom, out to lunch if I can swing it. Sometimes I just pop in the headphones with the answering machine recordings—the coffee date, the pickle ball, the renter and her barking dog—and point to my ears like I'm too busy doing all this work stuff. Each time he comes over, he has to walk past Tad's desk to mine and each time I feel a clench in my chest that I hate.

I feel like Sal is angling for that third date— determined not to drink too much and to make it happen. As for me, I wonder who makes these stupid dating rules. Do normal people really want to get it on at only the third interaction with someone? At least in that way I'm not basic. Instead, I'm an outlier, a weirdo.

I shuffle several drawings of hands together. Glancing through them I realize that I haven't drawn Sal's—not once. Even though he's got beautiful hands—long, broad fingers, square, trim nails. And even though I've drawn just about every other hand that had crossed my desk (some people take a meditation class; I sketch fingers). The omission glares at me and in it, and my new run-to-the-restroom habit, I realize that I've got to break up with Sal. Another stupid rule—that we should have to "break up" after only two formal interactions called dates. But I don't make the rules.

I determine that the next time he comes to my desk, I'll hear the invite, break the news. *I'm so sorry. I guess I'm not over my divorce, and I'm just not able to be all the way here right now.* Just thinking the words makes the knot in my stomach unwind a bit. Next time he comes over, I'll stay. I'll tell him.

But he doesn't come over. Not today. Instead, a bouquet of flowers does.

Every eye in the office follows the lilies and roses as they make their way to my desk. It takes every inch of willpower I have not to slump down into my seat.

From across the room, I catch Sal's eye, and he winks. I force the corners of my mouth up, then pluck the card from the arrangement. I need something to look at. Even if that thing is words I don't want to read. "Hello, beautiful. I'd be honored to have you as my guest at the police gala. Say yes."

Welp, now it seems a little harder to say 'no.' I let my gaze swim over the word 'gala.' It's in a week and a half, and it's the type of event girls like me aren't made for. With Rachel gone, I don't even have a friend to help me choose a dress.

Tad's head is tipped toward my desk. And I wonder what my short, clipped breaths are telling him.

CHAPTER 20

I arrive at the fertility clinic early, but stay in my car. I want to have a chance to pull myself together, gather my courage.

Fertility clinics make me think of Rachel. And thinking of Rachel makes me remember there's no Rachel anymore.

I suck in a quivery breath on the thought, try to picture Gabby and her chocolate cake with chocolate ice cream—all the good things that happened sandwiched between fertility treatments and cancer treatments, all the silver linings when I'd rather have a silver-filled cloud.

I'm not the only one gathering courage. In the other cars around me, I see people sitting and taking deep breaths too. It's that kind of place. In the car next to me, a woman presses un-ringed fingers over swollen eyes while a different couple walks in together, both with arms folded over their chests like they've had an argument.

A place where dreams blossom or die. Nothing in between.

A car pulls right up to the entrance and I know it's Tad. No one else in this entire clinic just pulls up and steps out.

I hear the door open, the soft plunk of his cane.

And now it's my turn, purse gathered, swig from my water bottle, quick message check on my phone. Keys in hand, door open, deliberate exit. The woman in the spot next to me has left, so Tad sees me, raises his hand in a wave.

The appointment is in two minutes. At least it can't be any more painful than that artist nephew and his stupid comments.

I'd never gone with Rachel to the fertility doctor, but she'd told me about it before she even talked with Aiden. She was bad about that —making big medical leaps without including her husband in the conversation. I mean, it's her body. But at a certain point she was going to need his assistance in the baby making. Least that's how my mama always explained it.

Anyway, the first time she went alone. The second time she took Aiden. After that she was sick for a full year. Puking, acne, diarrhea, all the things. Not all at once (usually), but a months-long succession of yuck. With no baby.

I couldn't have done it. Alex and I were already struggling and I couldn't imagine wanting a baby that much. I guess what I really couldn't imagine was a family functional enough that I wanted to add to it. The word 'baby' probably would have made Alex break out in hives. Marriage to a bona fide adult was already way more responsibility than he could handle.

The secretary at the clinic is a wisp of a woman—all bones and floating hair like it has some kind of fairy code it adheres to. She smiles broadly at Tad before checking her appointment book. I smile broadly back and she squints at me.

"They'll call you when the doctor is ready," she says, gesturing to the waiting area.

Tad and I nod. I suppose that we look nervous enough to fit right in with everyone else at the clinic.

We sit on squeaky chairs. I fidget. Tad leans over and whispers, "Think we can pull this off?"

"If Anderson finds out he'll kill us. I'm not even sure if this is ethical."

Tad shrugs. "Just a couple learning about their options. There's nothing illegal in that."

"I didn't say 'illegal,'" I reply.

And on that word, they call us back.

*D*r. Matthews is shorter than I am, decidedly stout—an adjective I'm not sure I've ever used before—and he is absolutely wearing a sweater vest. So either a psychopathic killer or someone with a bowl of peppermints on his coffee table. Could you be both? I'm pondering the question when he plunks down on a little chair and gazes at us. "Alrighty then, what's the problem?"

I clear my throat. We haven't exactly practiced and I'm realizing that we definitely should have practiced. We did map out a little scenario, and I begin. "We've been trying to have a baby for about six months now. And, well, nothing."

He nods. "Have you been monitoring your ovulation?"

I blink.

"Is it regular?" he asks.

"How?" I begin, clearing my throat again. "How do I, uh, monitor that?"

He looks at me in a squinty sort of way that seems to ask if I've met the internet. But instead of asking that, he says with a sort of pained patience, "Ideally, a woman ovulates around the middle of her menstrual cycle, usually between days eleven and seventeen. Of course, that's with a regular twenty-eight-day cycle." Here he looks at me as if he's asking if I'm regular, although he doesn't say the words. I feel confident that he will if I wait too long, that he'll be willing to spell out a whole lot of other stuff as well. I guess that's his job.

"I'm fairly regular," I pipe up. Tad tilts, always listening to everything.

"That's good," he says. "If you have a somewhat regular cycle you can take some natural measures to check for ovulation. For example, when a woman ovulates her temperature will spike somewhat. Take it in the morning before you get out of bed, and you'll get a fairly good idea of when you're the most fertile."

I stare at him, wondering if Tad knows any of

this, though I don't dare glance at him. Truly, high school sex ed has failed me. How did I not know this?

"If it seems that you are ovulating regularly, then we can run some tests on both of you to check for other issues. We could take a semen sample, check sperm counts…"

This time I do steal a glance at Tad and realize we are both in way, way over our heads.

Dr. Matthews is prattling on, but he's lost me, so naturally I interrupt. "Okay, I'll start to measure that. Is there, uh, anything else we should be doing?"

The doctor laughs. "Well, this probably goes without saying, but once you're aware of when you're ovulating, you two need to be sure you're having sex at those times. If you do regularly and things still don't work out, that's when I really need to get involved."

Tad smiles the tightest smile I've ever seen, and I forget the scenario, forget everything, just plow ahead like a lunatic.

"Yeah," I say. "Getting people involved is the tricky part, right?"

He shrugs, still smiling.

"Our friends," I say, "the Samuelsons—they were patients of yours too—recommended you actually. Anyway, so sad."

He nods, looking truly sorry, but also slightly uncomfortable.

But before he can change the subject, I charge ahead. "They, um, they were talking about a sperm donor. I'm not sure if they'd brought it up with you or not…" I trail off.

Dr. Matthews gets a bit of a blank look on his face, like he shut the blinds. "I was very sorry to hear about the Samuelsons," he says. "But I really can't discuss their medical care."

Of course he can't, HIPAA and stuff. "Oh, yes, of course," I say. "I just meant that it must be awful for you having to navigate that sort of thing with your patients. Bringing in surrogates and donors and things."

"It's usually quite smooth," he says, in a way that is also quite smooth. "A decision that has been coming for some time." I watch his hands. They don't twitch or fidget. They're chubby, chubby enough to have dimples at the knuckles. With nails gnawed to stubs, which only make the fingers look shorter.

Tad nods, and tilts. "How long, usually, before such a choice is made?"

"Often a few years," the doctor says.

I nod vigorously, thinking of Rachel and Aiden.

"So I don't suppose it's something we need to talk about today."

"Not at all," the doctor says.

"Macie has been pretty nervous about this," he says, putting a hand on my knee. I feel the heat of his hand, those long fingers, the gentle pressure. Even if we had had a script, I would have forgotten it.

"Erm," I murmur intelligently.

"I'm actually the one who suggested coming in," Tad continues. "She was a little anxious about the whole thing."

The doctor is wearing a look that says that is pretty obvious.

"She was worried because our friends, well, sometimes the fertility issues just brought up a little drama. You know how it does."

The doctor nods, like he does indeed know. "Fertility treatments can be very hard on couples. That's why we start out as naturally as possible."

Tad and I nod together like an actual couple. "And I do encourage people to take it slowly and know their own limits." He gives me a pointed look. "I've seen plenty of couples so in love they're willing to fork out a full year's salary to share a baby, and then they end up divorced when all is said and done."

Tad quirks that eyebrow.

"What a horrible job you must have," I say without meaning to.

Tad leans back, like he's given up on trying to help me.

"More often wonderful," the doctor corrects. "You two go home and try a few more natural methods. If nothing has worked in six more months, come back and we'll talk."

"Thank you for your time, Doctor," Tad says.

"Gladly," he answers, standing and shaking both of our hands. "I wish you luck."

"Thank you," Tad says.

We're gonna need it. I don't say it, for once. But here we are. Back to square one. No hints, no leads.

* * *

"Okay, so we're officially the worst married couple ever," Tad says.

"Ouch," I add, making a joke of it, though I do feel a little pang at the words. "And not true. Trust me."

Tad opens his mouth to say something and then doesn't. "Anyway," he finally says, opening his phone to call for a ride. "Do you think it was a random crime?"

"Awfully clever crime to be random."

"A murder-suicide, then. Like Anderson thinks."

"He does not," I say, beeping the lock on my car. "Not really."

"Only because we got into his head. He's going to tell us the murder-suicide is the only thing that makes sense." On the last phrase, he does a spot-on imitation of Anderson's voice.

"Wow," I say. "Didn't know you could do that."

"I'm a man of many talents."

In the distance a dog barks. We both stop talking, look to the sound.

"But he's wrong," Tad murmured. "A murder-suicide is the only thing that doesn't make any sense at all."

CHAPTER 21

Tad scoots into my passenger seat without asking. I look at him, confused.

"Follow that dog," he says gallantly.

"We're not even close to the Samuelsons' house."

"Okay, not that dog, but let's look around the Samuelsons' neighborhood. I wish we knew what a poodle sounded like."

"Google 'poodle' and listen to its bark," I say, turning left and heading to the suburbs.

Tad does and for several minutes we listen to YouTube videos of barking dogs. I guarantee I could *not* pick it out from another dog, though maybe Tad could.

Tad clicks off his phone and laughs softly to himself.

"What?" I say.

"You know, when I was a kid, the girl next door had this pet duck."

"Duck?" I ask.

"Yeah, there was this huge pond at the end of our road and this duck had been abandoned and my neighbor had rescued it and nursed it back to health. Anyway, this girl—"

"The girl next door," I say with a smile.

"Of course," he replies and I can tell he's smiling too.

"So she had this duck she found in her yard when it was a baby—quacking away or the baby equivalent of a quack, a squeak. But its mother never came. The duckling was just pacing her yard. So she took it a little mashed up corn, put out a bowl of water."

"Like a dog?" I say.

"Kind of, except soon she was feeding it bugs and worms and spinach and stuff. It would eat out of her hands, splash around in the little dish she set out. They did this for weeks. She named it. It slept by the back door. And then one day it was gone."

I raise my eyebrows. "And?" I say.

"I'd just gotten my diagnosis about a year earlier. For my eyes."

"Wait," I say. "You could see before that?"

"I can sort of see now," he says.

"I know," I say, "but I mean…" It feels rude to finish the sentence.

"*See* see," he says, finishing for me.

"Yeah," I mumble.

"Yes, my vision was normal until about eight. By ten, I was more or less where I am now."

"So you were that age, the girl lost her duck. Go on."

"I didn't have a ton of friends at this point. Not like now when I'm just drowning in them…"

And it takes me a minute to hear the joke in his voice. I smile—I hadn't pegged him as the self-effacing type.

He laughs. "Anyway, it was even worse then. My mom had pulled me out of school to homeschool me and we were waiting for a spot to open in this special school an hour away. A school for the blind." He scowls.

"Were the kids mean about it? Your diagnosis?" I ask.

"Not mostly. Mostly they just went on with their kid stuff while I was trapped at home. But anyway, I heard this girl crying one day and I put my good eye up to the fence and she was sitting on the back stoop just bawling."

"And you offered to help."

"Of course. So we wandered the neighborhood.

But there were loads of ducks and quacks. But then I had an idea. She had these home videos. I mean, her parents must have thought the whole duckling thing was adorable—so we watched a couple. The duck looked like an adult at the end, and it had this really loud quack."

"You found it," I say.

"By listening," he finishes. "My first foray into my current career. And the first time I realized how powerful just listening can be." He pauses. "But I had to hear it first. I couldn't just pick it out."

"You still friends with that girl?" I ask.

"On Facebook," he says. "And she's still kind of a crazy animal person. She has a YouTube channel with weird animal stories—inspiring stuff. It's pretty popular."

"How popular?" I ask.

"Enough to pay the rent," he says.

"What's it called?"

"Crazy duck lady."

"Fitting," I say. "I'm guessing with a name like that she's still single."

"Not even close," he says. "The good ones never are."

"Thanks a lot," I say.

"You're not single," he replies. "Even a blind guy could see those flowers from Sal. Flashy."

Yes, they were. Very nice, very sweet, but definitely flashy—all roses and lilies and peony and I don't know what else.

"Look her up," I say in order to divert this wayward conversation. I roll into the Samuelsons' neighborhood, watching the neat houses that march forward. The Samuelsons are the seventh down.

"Computer," he says. It's his voice command and it's kind of funny. "Sally Mae. Crazy duck lady. Youtube."

Obediently, his phone finds the video and it starts to play. Today's story is an interview with a family whose dog got lost on a family vacation. Nine months later, across 1800 miles and ten states, it found its way back to their doorstep.

"Amazing," Sally Mae is saying and you can hear the actual dog yapping in the background. "Animals have the most fantastic internal mapping systems." She goes on with a few more questions, but Tad and I aren't listening.

"It must be dead," he says, pursing his lips tightly at the words.

"Or trapped," I add, listening to Sally Mae thank her guest as I pull up to the Samuelsons' house.

Tad turns to me, his whole body. "Yes. Or trapped."

CHAPTER 22

I drop Tad off at his house, still chewing on that thought.

Chewing. Just like a trapped dog. And then I click 'humane society' in my maps.

"Any new dogs?" I ask when John looks up from his desk.

"Back so soon," he answers. I'm pleased that he recognizes me.

"We got one this morning, but I'm not sure he's what you're looking for."

"Why not?" I ask.

"Great Dane mix."

"Oh," I answer, gazing at the cats.

"Close to 200 pounds," he says.

"Dear glory," I respond, accidentally walking toward a cage with kittens.

"Perhaps something smaller, then," John answers, and there's something in his tone. What is it?

He's unlocking the cage and before I know it a six-month tabby is in my arms.

"How are the allergies?" he asks, giving me a look.

I sniffle, or at least sniff. "Uh, good," I say.

He nods. And I realize what the tone was—used car salesman. The tabby is gazing at me. I'm gazing back. I shake my head. I'm here for dogs. Well, dog. "I was wondering if I could pick up another dog walking form," I say, stroking the kitten.

"Sure," he says.

"I lost mine," I lie. Pretty sure it's still sitting on my passenger seat.

"Right," he answers, shuffling through some papers as I tickle the cat's neck.

John comes up with the paper. I part from the tabby, and when it's gone, my arms feel kind of empty and cold.

John walks with me to the door and hands me the paper. Just before I leave, I notice a few rabbits in little cages, and even one hedgehog. "Cool," I say.

"Aren't they? Brand new. We've even got a couple of birds. I'll show you."

When he says a couple, he means a *couple*. Two lovebirds in the same cage, one leaning onto the breast of the other like they're about to watch a movie together, a sad movie. The way they huddle, well, they don't have doleful eyes, but you can kind of tell this isn't their forever home, or furrever home, as one of the promotional signs reads.

"Just got these beauties a few days ago," John says. "No one got rid of them, but their owner passed. It's not uncommon with birds because they live so long. And sometimes when birds have been with someone for a while, they get depressed when that person is gone. They can even start to pluck at their own feathers. But since these two have each other, I think they'll be okay. And at least they're used to the idea of a cage."

I think of my cold, empty arms, of Bernard alone somewhere, his owners dead; and I want to tell John that he's bumming me out on every possible level. Instead when he asks if I want to feed them, I say, "Sure." Because what else am I going to say?

He hands me a little square of pressed seed and I angle it through the cage. At first, the birds just gaze at me, then one bobs down, making a grab. It's so sudden that I'm not prepared for it and end up dropping the rest of the seed square through the slats. The other bird looks at me, makes a noise that sounds distinctly like a scold, or maybe a laugh.

"They like you," John says.

"I think they're making fun of me," I answer.

"Not sure there's much difference with birds," he says, then turns to coo at the birds, "Huh, you two?" The smaller—female, I'd guess, with my brilliant understanding of the animal kingdom—coos a little sound while her mate goes to retrieve some seed from the square.

"Oh, they'll go quick," John says. "Two lovelies like these."

I hope he's right, but they're not going to go quick to me, even though John suggests it at least twice in the next three minutes before I leave. Two lovebirds—that's the last thing I need to come home to every day.

⁂

Speaking of lovebirds, when I get in my car and check my phone, I see that Sal has texted me twice, asking what color my dress is for the gala so he can match his tie. I am so out of my league. I haven't even thought about my dress, much less *his* tie. And I suppose there will be flowers or a boutonniere to worry about too. I didn't realize I was signing up for Homecoming 101. I take a breath, fingers hovering over my phone. "Going shopping tomorrow. I'll let you know then." I add a smiley face to show my sheer eagerness. Then lean my head against my headrest, and groan.

CHAPTER 23

So...dress shopping. Or maybe the word is *gown*, since this is a *gala* and all. Anyway, since I don't own a dress of any variety, gown or otherwise, it seems like the type of thing you should do with a friend. Trouble is, I don't have one. I had Rachel—yeah, yeah, we all know that by now. And I like Aiden's sister, Kate, though she might be even worse at dress shopping than I am. A few good friends from high school and college—all in different states now. But otherwise, I'm a little dry in the girlfriend department. I'm friends online with a few of the other girls from the dentist's office, but it would feel weird to call them up. Same with a few of the wives of Alex's old friends. In fact, I got along fairly well with a lot of Alex's friends, not just their wives, so there are people. Just no one...close. When

I think about it, Tad is probably the closest friend I've got now; and something about that makes me really, really sad.

Except there isn't time for that. Right now there's only time to put on the big girl panties and remember I'm a strong independent woman who can, in fact, go dress shopping alone, even if she hasn't been to the mall for approximately seven thousand years. Why the mall, you ask? Well, I'm not nearly sophisticated enough to know of anywhere else, and I don't dare risk a dress online with some size two, six-foot model showing me how great everything's going to fit. No. I need to stand in a dressing room with my socks on, fluorescent lights glaring, and see if the dress can pass that test.

I start at Macy's. It seems a safe, mid-level bet.

I overestimate my shopping skill level. I know one thing—no pink. That includes corals, mauves, roses—it's just not my thing. Blue always feels safe. And I kind of like green, but it seems like it's not in style this year because there's nothing on the racks except one strapless number that reminds me of a mermaid. I'm not a mermaid.

I wander the entirety of the rest of the mall— from teen stores to stores for mature women. I try on one dress without straps (out!) and one dress with a suit coat (also totally out!). Then it's back to Macy's so I can get to my car, but on the way a saleswoman is putting up a new display. I pause. She glances at me. "Can I help you?"

I almost shake my head no, but I mean, I do need help. "I've been invited to a police gala," I say.

"Ooooh, that sounds exciting."

I force a smile.

"Boyfriend, or new flame?" she asks.

"Neither," I reply.

"Friend?" she asks.

"Also, not quite," I reply, realizing that I should have fled when I had the chance.

"Mmmm, that's a tricky place," she says, sifting through the dresses, slinky fabric slipping through her fingers. "I've been there though. Nothing too sexy or too dowdy, too bright or too dull. Essentially, the perfect dress. Honestly, it's a lot easier if someone is just looking for a little action."

And I know I shouldn't, but I sort of snort a laugh. I mean, it's funny. And it probably is a lot easier.

"But you didn't hear that from me."

"My ears are sealed. Also, if we could keep it under $200, that'd be a bonus." I'm almost bluffing here, because $200 is going to be really, really hard for me to pull off.

"So…the perfect dress. Nothing mini. Less than

$200. Lucky for you, I enjoy a good challenge. And even luckier, we just got a new shipment in."

She scoots a box to her side. She's just hung a sequined navy dress. I can see the price tag and it's close to $500.

"No peeking," she says when I try peering into the box. "This one is all navy and blues, but there's another…" She whips out a box cutter like a martial arts master and whirls around to a smaller box, slitting it open with such skill that I almost step back.

The first dress she pulls out—it's like a waterfall, falling over and through her fingers. "Gray?" I say.

"Silver," she replies.

I guess silver is a thing you can be when you're a gown.

"I don't know," I begin.

"It's not pink," she says as if she's been reading my mind. "And I think it'd look amazing with your hair, those eyes, and that perfect, clear skin."

I'm not sure which girl she's talking about, but that top dress will never work. "Not that one," I say. "Pretty sure I'd have to invest in some Spanx, maybe even buy out the company to wear that thing."

She sets the waterfall aside. "No shame in Spanx," she replies. "But if you want to keep it simpler, then maybe something like this."

And, I mean, maybe. It's also silver and when she

shoves the dress into my hand, I have to admit that the color does kind of fit with my skin. It's not stiff, but not as flowy as the other one. It's in one piece with no cut-outs.

"And look," she says. "It has these beautiful accents."

By accents she means shimmery lines of—I don't know the word, but something like embroidery running along the neckline, wrists, and hem. I have to admit I kind of like it.

"Price," I say, turning it over in my hands.

"Go try it on first," she says.

"You know I can just look at the price—" I begin.

"Just don't," she says. "Try it on; see what you think."

This is definitely not the way my mother told me to do it. She would check the price first on everything, probably faster than her brain could register the color.

I huff out a sigh, just like a teenager, and the woman smiles. Evil genius that she is. I can already tell the dress is going to fit, just by looking at it; just by holding it. Hopefully it doesn't cost five hundred bucks because perfect or not, I just can't fork that much out right now, and I'll be forced to show up to the gala looking like a mermaid, or the mother at a wedding.

Once in the dressing room, I shake the dress fully long. It comes to my ankles with those pretty accents flowing around. The sleeves are tighter up top with flowy cuffs, but they're not so long that I'll have to drag them through the salmon or whatever dish they serve. The neck is a deep oval, almost square, but a little softer. I wriggle out of my jeans and slip it over my head. It's soft and just a little stretchy. No zipper —that's kind of a relief.

And then, there I am—a silvery princess. She's right. The color is just right with my hair, good for my eyes, great for my skin. Why have I not been wearing silver every day of my entire life? I do something I've never done before, even though it's the most basic move of all womanhood. I take out my phone and snap a picture of myself in the mirror. Oh, I'm not sharing that sucker with anyone. I just kind of want to remember what I looked like all glitzed out, rocking a metallic shade, looking like I could walk a red carpet, or at least some color of carpet. Before I crush this beautiful moment by glancing at the price tag.

I glance up at the fluorescent lights, gathering my strength, then slip the bit of paper out of the sleeve. It's not $200. Closer to $250.

I slither out of the dress, re-clothe—feeling a lot like Cinderella must have after that last stroke of twelve. I drape the dress reverently over my arm, and remember how Alex never cared about his budget at all and how I was the one who always had to deal with the consequences of that.

"So," the saleslady—Gretchen is the name on the tag—asks when I emerge.

"You're good," I say.

"Oh, I knew that already," she answers.

"It fits; it's beautiful."

"But…"

"It's over $200."

"By a mere twenty-five percent."

"Yes," I say, doing the math.

"And if you sign up for a credit card today you'll get twenty percent off all purchases, plus an instant $10 off delivered to your email."

I peck at the numbers in my head. The twenty percent alone takes it down to $200, with an extra ten to grow on.

"I don't need another credit card," I say.

"Just pay off the dress and cancel it."

"I could be a credit card addict, drowning in debt, and you would just feed my addiction like this?" I wave my arm with the dress hanging off of it for emphasis; it sparkles under the lights.

"Only for a dress like that." She laughs. "Also,

people who try to look at the price tag first are usually not deeply in credit card debt."

"Depends on their ex-husbands," I reply, though the truth is that I got Alex's debts paid back within six months of the divorce.

"Are you deeply in credit card, or any other, type of debt?"

"No."

She smirks. "Just buy the dress."

"Fine," I say.

She walks me over to a cash register, digs out the credit card paperwork, and we're in business.

After she's wrapped the dress in tissue paper (I've legitimately never bought a piece of clothing that has been wrapped in tissue paper), she leans over the register counter. "Look, I'm probably not allowed to do this at work, but I also sell a few cosmetics on the side. I'm hosting a party this Tuesday. You should come."

I hesitate. Cosmetics. Another foreign word—kind of like 'gown.'

"First makeover's free."

"I don't know," I say.

"Have I ever done you wrong?" she asks.

I laugh. "I guess everyone deserves a second chance."

She smiles and I have to admit that her own makeup looks just right.

I take the card she hands me—a fat lipstick next to her name.

"See you Tuesday, Macie," she says.

I wander to my car in a bit of a daze. Is it possible that in one hour I have succeeded in procuring both a dress—excuse me, *gown*—and a friend? I glance at the card. Gretchen Michaels.

The party's at 6:00 on Tuesday. It's not like I have any other plans.

I can't resist a stop to the humane society on my way home. It's just easier to feel your feelings when you're surrounded by furry creatures. Today, maybe I will even help John walk a dog. I've got the energy for that. Of course, it'd be nice if he'd gotten a new dog, the *right* dog, but at this point that has started to feel like a bit of an impossibility.

I ask anyway.

"No new dogs today," he says.

"Anything else new?" I say. It's a question I don't need to ask. I mean, I'm here to find out about a dog. Obviously.

Which is why I find myself cuddling a chinchilla—the newest addition to the humane society. It's maybe the softest thing I've ever touched, and I say so.

That might have been a mistake because John goes into hard sales mode.

"Easy to feed," he says. "Simple diets. Great for working people. Oh, and they don't produce many allergens. So…good for people with allergies."

I nod at each selling point, but when he raises his eyebrows at the end, I shake my head.

"Just a dog, huh?" he says, eyes narrowing like he's trying to look into my soul.

"For now," I reply in a dodgy way.

He tickles the chinchilla's neck. "They're not the cuddliest, but they enjoy being with their owners."

I nod again. I can't seem to help myself.

He looks sideways at me. "Everyone wants a dog," he says, re-caging the chinchilla and grabbing a mop. "But not you, sweetie. I think you just like the company."

And something about that—that true statement so honestly, basically stated—it just makes me want to cry.

"Thanks so much, John. I've got to go."

"See you next time, hun. We'll find you the right match."

I smile weakly. Then race to my car.

CHAPTER 24

One last trip to the house before Anderson gives the green light for people to come in and clean it, for that bright 'For Sale' sign to pop up in the lawn.

None of us knows what we're looking for, but Anderson is the only one who whines about this fact. "We've got to get this closed," he keeps saying. "If there was ever a case here, it's surely gone cold by now."

I look over at Tad. He's tapping away, an annoyed rhythm. I wish I could join him somehow—some type of secret code—the tap tap version of a shared eye roll.

When we get inside, everything is absolutely exactly like it's always been. Anderson indulges himself in his own little eye roll.

I wander through the kitchen, retracing our steps, our thoughts. I take in the dog dish, the matched set of mugs, take pictures with my mind—pictures I sometimes wish I could shake away. Then I make my way to the bedroom, which looks almost meticulously untouched. Bed made, dressers clean, dust the only thing living here now. And there's something so impossibly sad about that fact. I sniffle—dust allergy, you know.

Tad has gone the opposite direction and I can hear him tapping his way into the living room. When he gets to the rug, the sound stops. I tilt toward the room, just like he does when he's listening hard. And then, his voice. "What's this?"

"It's an answering machine," Anderson says, flat, annoyed.

"Have you checked it?" Tad asks.

From Anderson's silence, I'm guessing that's a no.

"Just like our first case," Tad mutters.

"What?" Anderson asks.

"Macie and I, our first case," Tad says. "Answering machine. That's how we—she—figured it out. Hey Macie, come here."

He clicks the button, skipping back over several telemarketing calls and something with that renter. Until he gets to the day of the murder. September

18th. There's only one message, and it's a familiar voice.

"I really hate to call you at home, Mel, but I'm not getting you on your cell. I've got to cancel coffee today, hun. Something came up."

Tad and I look at each other.

It's a very Kentucky accent. But whose? And does it even matter?

"That voice," Tad says. "Do we know it from somewhere?"

"Sure," I say. "From the other phone message."

"No," he replies. "Somewhere else. The way she said that 'hun'—there's something about it. So familiar."

"Familiar?" Anderson and I both ask together—probably the first time *that's* ever happened.

"Maybe you bumped into her at Walmart," Anderson says, meaning it as an insult.

But with Tad's ear it's a definite possibility.

Tad taps at the answering machine. "Macie, grab that for me, will you?"

"You can't just steal stuff from the house," Anderson says.

"I'm not stealing; it's just the first purchase for the estate sale. He pulls a hundred from his wallet. "Seems fair, don't you think?"

"Seems dumb," Anderson answers, but I can tell

he's intrigued, even though he doesn't want to be. "Also, I'm looking the other way because I don't want to know what you two do."

And he literally turns the other way so he can't see.

"Do me a favor, Anderson," Tad says as I fiddle with the answering machine, pulling out the cord.

"This whole investigation is a favor to you," Anderson grumbles.

"Great. Then add one to my tab. Don't let the chief close the case until we figure out who belongs to that voice."

"You might never figure it out," Anderson says.

"We will," Tad replies.

Anderson rolls his eyes, but he doesn't say no. It's then that I realize he's in it just as much as we are. Okay, maybe not just as much, but close. The only difference is that he doesn't want to be, doesn't even know why he is. But he knows the murder-suicide is off, and he knows something about Tad is on. He just—we don't—quite know what yet.

CHAPTER 25

I thought a cosmetics party would be the worst thing in the world, but it's only really like the half worst thing in the world. There's free food, so that's a win. And the free food tastes good, maybe not quite ex-Alex good, but it's home-made and the cookies are moist and the quiche isn't runny. What more could you ask for? Gretchen's also got cocktails, which I pass on. It's best to know when you're a lightweight, though it becomes quickly clear that several of the women do not realize they're lightweights. Kind of a brilliant marketing plan, really. Because about sixty minutes in, I'm pretty sure the drunk girls have bought at least half of Gretchen's inventory. I'm still trying to settle on a lip gloss so I don't seem like a rude cookie freeloader.

Gretchen sees me and smiles. "Skip the gloss, Macie. Get yourself a real red to go with that dress."

"You're crazy," I say.

"Here, try this one," she says, ignoring my objection.

I stubbornly purse my lips together. "No way. I'm not wearing red lipstick. It's like the most un-me thing in the world."

"Put that color on and tell me it's not you."

"Fine," I say as the other ladies apply blush and gossip about their husbands. I splotch it onto my lips as carelessly as I can manage and Gretchen shoves a mirror into my face. I stop, look at the stranger staring back at me. I mean, it's still very un-me, or at least un-the-person-I-think-of-as-me. But it does look good. On that person in the mirror, whoever she is. Really good. I just, well maybe I stare for a minute. Then my brain catches up to my face.

"Nope, not me," I say pushing the mirror away.

Gretchen cocks a perfectly lined eyebrow. "Buy a gloss and I'll give it to you for free."

"You don't have to give it to me free…"

"I won't. It's with a gloss. This one." She shoves a gloss at me that I haven't tried yet—kind of a plum color that seems too purple, but isn't when I actually put it on my face.

I shake my head. "How?"

"I'm good with color," she says.

"I'll buy the red too," I say.

"Nope, you won't," she says. "Consider it a free sample. From someone who knows she'll get a repeat customer."

"I'll probably only wear it to the gala," I insist.

She smiles, though it's more of a 'we'll see' sort of smirk. I take another cookie.

CHAPTER 26

$\mathcal{I}$'m getting ready for work, by which I mean putting the lipstick on and wiping it off again, when I hear the voice. The voice from the answering machine, only smoother, less southern. It's coming from my TV.

In the other room, I've got some morning show running—a knock off of *The View*— with a bunch of ladies who sit around talking about random political issues or the latest fashions or how to make a great Super Bowl spread. Today it's a national clothing drive. I'm desperately wiping lipstick off my face and they're chit chatting about collecting bras and underwear for women's shelters. One of the hosts is talking about how important this is because women's shelters are always constantly short on underwear. Then the voice again. I rush into the living room, and stop.

Because right there next to the host, Sandra Stevens, is a buxom blond wearing nothing more than a red bra and panties to match. If they could even be called 'panties,' not 'stringies.' I shake my head. Maybe I misunderstood and they're really talking about the latest Victoria's Secret show or something. But then Sandra goes on about how to contribute and how much benefit it will bring the women, and the guest—the voice from the phone messages—she's standing up (I can't unsee it) and walking her lace and string adorned buttocks over to a display of the most ridiculously impractical lingerie known to womankind. The charity is hers—her baby, she calls it, and I hear that twang, the one she's mostly covered up—but who is she? The other women, they're calling her Tiffani. Tiffani who? I shake my head, close my eyes. I don't need thongs or lace or charities. I just need the voice. Yes, it's definitely the one. Coffee, at noon. A place called Beanstalk.

I open my eyes. She's seated again and stroking a pile of silk panties. And then the name of the charity comes up. Cane's Closet. And then it all clicks together. Cane. Tiffani Cane. Of course. Arthur's wife. Wealthy, beautiful, scantily clad. In-law to the Samuelsons.

And—excuse me while I judge a book by the cover, or very obvious lack of cover—but she seems like exactly the type of woman that might be able to seduce and/or kill someone (when she's not providing free, if impractical, underclothing to the needy). Because, like, who besides a total psychopath could get up on national television to talk about charity wearing only underwear?

I text Tad, still staring at the screen, trying to get the number for the charity down on my phone. And then, accidentally, I call it. And then there I am on the phone making a donation of $20 to Cane's Closet, because what on earth else am I supposed to do? It's for the women's shelters, for Pete's sake. And then Tad texts back, "How are we going to talk to her?" And then the woman on the line says, "You're the 3000th caller. Congratulations."

"Congratulations?" I ask.

"Yeah," she answers. "Every 1000th person gets to attend a zoom call with Ms. Cane."

"Zoom call?" I croak.

"Yes, she's agreed to do ten personal consults."

"Consults?" I whisper, worried that I know what's coming next. I do.

"Yes," the woman says. "She'll help you know

what type of undergarment is best for your body type. It's her thing, after all."

I nod stupidly at the phone.

"Outerwear optional," the woman chirps.

But before I can roll over and die, she gives me the time for the call. Tomorrow. Noon, Eastern time.

Tad is texting me furiously. Apparently he's tuned in to the show as well.

I text him back, delete, text again. I have no words. *Don't worry. I've won an underwear consultation.* Delete delete delete.

"Man, I wish I could see better," he says and I picture him with his eye right up to the TV. He sends me a string of laughing emojis (I'm not laughing). Then, "Maybe Anderson can get an interview." Then another text. "Though she's clearly in New York right now."

"I think I know someone she works with," I say. It's only mostly a lie. "I just called her, actually."

"Really, who?" Tad asks.

"Her secretary," I say.

"You didn't mention this before?"

"I didn't make the connection," I reply. "But anyway, she's gonna try to set up a zoom call or something."

"Really?" he texts. "When?"

"Hopefully tomorrow," I text.

"That's great. Let me know what time, and I'll be there."

"Sure," I say. But that one's a complete lie. I'm going to accidentally give him the wrong time for sure.

"Great work, Macie," he texts. "You're kind of amazing."

And I feel the blush—rising hot from my neck to my forehead. The only question is whether it's from Tad's compliment or my upcoming 'outerwear optional' consultation.

CHAPTER 27

Tad calls early the next morning. "Did you get that zoom call?"

"Why?" I ask.

"Because," he says. "I just found this. The recommitment ceremony—it happened right before Mrs. Cooper died. And her death wasn't a total surprise—terminal cancer. The Canes said they wanted to do it before she was gone."

"They expected to be included in the will."

"*She* expected to be included in the will," Tad said. "And judging from her string of lovers, and then the expense of the recommitment ceremony, it seems she would have been mightily disappointed that she wasn't."

"It's still conjecture," I say.

"Yes," he replies. "Which is why it'll be great to be there for that call. Did you get a time set up?"

I clear my throat, fish for some words. "One," I say.

"Great," he replies. "Let's meet at the diner for it."

"I think it'd be better with just me," I reply.

"I won't be seen," he adds. "Don't worry about that."

Oh, that's not what I'm worried about.

***

She's wearing clothes. Business-y ones even. The irony. Her accent is kind of subtle when she first comes on, just like it was for the TV show, but when she hears my drawl, she lets go and all the Kentucky comes through. "Where you from, hun?"

I should probably make something up, but I'm just too nervous. "Swallowsville," I say. "It's just west of Louisville."

"Oh, I know, baby. Grew up near there myself. Small world, ain't it?"

"So small," I answer.

"Well, baby. We've only got forty minutes, so let's get hoppin'."

Yeah, hoppin'.

"I'm gonna need you to get a measuring tape and the tightest t-shirt you got if you want to keep one on. Lose the bra if you can. We want an accurate measurement."

I nod, stupidly, then don't move.

She gazes at me through the screen. "Don't be shy, honey. We're both women. Part of the problem with getting the correct sizes for undergarments is that women tend to get measured in stores where they're fully clothed." Then—my face must be horrified—"Listen. Just go in the bathroom and I'll tell you what measurements you need. You get them, and come back."

I nod, slip out of my chair. Do I have a measuring tape? I hope so, because I don't even know enough about my size to take a guestimate.

Fortunately, my junk drawer comes through for me, and about five minutes later I'm back in front of the zoom call with a piece of scrap paper in hand.

"Perfect, honey," she coos. "Now that wasn't so bad, was it?"

Mmmm, it was kind of bad. I'm not exactly thrilled with my measurements, but she really is all business. "Okay, hon, this is what you need."

She gives me a size I never would have chosen for myself, suggests a type, and even a few brands that she supports. "These are good for bustier girls."

"Bustier?" I ask weakly.

"Of course, curvy girls like yourself," she replies. "When you want to add a little more hourglass from waist to chest, it's the perfect thing."

"Perfect," I say, with maybe the saddest smile ever known to zoom.

"Oh, sugar," she says, letting the south drip through. "Don't you worry. Curvy girls have so much more to work with than flat ones. You just have to suck the curves up into the right places. You don't need to create a dang thing. Thank your stars for that."

Yeah, I'll be sure to do that.

"Maybe I should head over to one of your husband's gyms to work off a few of these curves." I laugh. It's a little forced, but passable.

She doesn't skip a beat, doesn't ask how I know about her husband and his businesses. "Oh honey, you don't need you no gym. You're gorgeous just like you are."

I feel my insides warm up just a bit. It takes a little more work to remind myself this is a potential killer seductress who dresses in red lace on national television.

"Must be nice though," I fish, "to have a husband with all those gyms."

"It ain't the worst," she says. "But between you

and me, honey, it's not the best either. All the cute butts that wander past that man. It's a wonder he's still with me."

Isn't it though? "Oh, he'd be an idiot to ever leave you," I gush. "Besides, didn't you guys do some big commitment ceremony a little while ago?"

She smiles and I can't tell if it's sincere or not. I find myself wishing Tad was here to read her voice a little better than I can do right now. "We did. It was so beautiful. Even his dying grandmamma made it out."

"Awww." I do my best to keep gushing, but gushing is not my greatest talent. "That's so sweet."

"She passed just after," Tiffani says.

"Oh no! How sad," I say.

"Art and I were pretty tore up over it, but we knew it was coming. Part of the reason we wanted to get the recommitment ceremony done."

"Of course," I say. But really, I know our session is almost done and I need more information. *And where were you on the morning of September 18th* seems like the wrong approach. "How's it been?" I ask. "The recommitment?"

She looks at me kind of sideways on the screen.

"I mean, it must have been hard with his grandmamma passing and all. You know how men are."

"Yeah," she says. "Yeah, I really do. And then Phil," she almost whispers.

And I know I'm not supposed to know, but I almost break. "Phil?" I say, my voice cracking.

She laughs. "I know what you're thinking. Another man, right?"

I mean, I would have been thinking just that if I didn't know who Phil was. I lean toward the zoom call.

"Listen, I'm only saying this 'cause you might hear it somewhere else since you're in Swallowsville. But Art's second cousin died just recently, his wife too."

"Both of them?" I ask, doing my best to sound incredulous. "Car accident?"

"No," she says. "Worse. Much worse. Another type of accident. Melanie and I were going to have coffee that morning. That exact morning…" Her voice trails off, just like in a movie, and I realize she's a better actress than I am. But my head is reeling. That morning, the morning she cancelled on the phone.

"What kind of accident?"

"Don't matter," she says, winding her own tape measure around her fingers. Long fingers, long nails. Right handed. "But it was real tragic. And we never got our coffee."

"How awful," I say and this time I mean it; I don't have to act.

She snaps the measuring tape and I almost jump. "Honey, I think our session's almost over and we've barely even discussed formal undergarments. I'm sorry. I just got carried away."

"Oh, that's okay," I say. "I don't go to a lot of formal events." Though one is coming up and I could use *some* advice. But I push that thought away. "I'm so sorry about your cousin."

"Second cousin," she says, cool as anything. "Second cousin-in-law." And then she laughs this bitter laugh. "You'd think it would have been me and Art—that kind of drama. Things never happen to the right people."

"What do you mean?" I say, trying my best to act like one of the girls instead of a weird responsible type.

"Never mind," she says. "Just seems like karma hasn't done them right."

"That's..." I hunt for the words. "I'm sorry."

"Me too, sugar."

Our session is about to time out, nearly forty minutes.

"You know where I was that morning—why I couldn't do coffee earlier?"

I lean in.

"Oh, honey, I wish I could have, would have. Then maybe Melanie would still be right here."

"No," I say. "You can't blame yourself like that. Accidents happen."

"Not this type of accident," she says.

"And where were you?" I ask, sincerely eager to know, and watching the counter on the zoom call. Two minutes.

"Well, it's no secret that Art and I were on the rocks."

"So you took a lover?" I ask, and I'm pretty sure it sounds like Jane Austen wrote that line, not someone currently living in a world not involving petticoats. "Is that why you couldn't do coffee earlier?"

She laughs and there's a sad edge to it—real or fake? I really need Tad here to pay better attention. "Oh no, honey. I went to a divorce attorney. And I don't recommend it. They're even more expensive than lovers, and a lot less fun."

"Wow," I say.

"Yeah, wow," she replies. "You see what I mean. Wrong karma."

"And who—" I start to ask. But then the timer is at five seconds and she's waving goodbye and making me swear to buy the type of bra she recommended and I swear it, and she blows me a kiss.

I'm sitting in the diner when Tad arrives.

"You're early," he said.

Funny thing about that. "You mean, you're late," I say. "It was at noon."

"You texted that it was at one," he says. "And you never sent me a text to tell me I was late. I would have hurried over." He leans toward me, listening for my voice.

"I was kind of busy," I say.

"You sent me the wrong time on purpose," he replies. "I can hear it in your voice."

His voice is hurt, or suspicious—a combination of both. "Why?"

I sigh, going for Tiffani's sweet drama and failing. "It was an underwear consultation. Tiffani Cane does this charity for giving homeless or sheltered women underwear and I donated and got a chance to talk to her, but it was a consultation."

Tad doesn't answer, but he tips away from me, back ramrod straight, every part of his body still. And then he laughs. This big, baritone sound. I didn't realize I and underwear were that hilarious, but whatever. "So what'd she recommend?"

"Really?" I say. "Or do you want to know what her alibi was?"

He straightens up. "You really got that from her?"

"I really did."

"Who is it?" he asks, distracted from bras for the time being.

"Divorce attorney," I say.

"That's great," he replies. "Which one?"

I clear my throat. We'd kind of gotten cut off before I got to that part.

He looks at me.

"Surely there aren't that many in Swallowsville."

"If it was in Swallowsville."

"It was," I say. "She was supposed to have coffee with Melanie Samuelson and didn't because of this appointment."

"They could have zoomed," he says. "It could be anyone."

"It wasn't," I reply. "Look, I'll call around and figure out who it was."

Tad tips his head to the side, the crack of a smile at his lips.

It takes me three hours. One hundred and two calls to different divorce attorneys, or rather their secretaries. One hundred and two times saying, "My friend, Tiffani, recommended your office. Tiffani Cane. Do you remember her?"

Until finally one takes the bait, answers, "Oh, yes, Ms. Cane."

And then we chat about my upcoming fake divorce, and I say I'll have to think about it and she tells me that any conversation with the attorney will cost $300 an hour. And I thank her.

I lean back in my chair, rubbing my temples for several minutes before texting Tad, "It's Dawson and Son. Have Anderson check the alibi."

After that, I pop a couple of Tylenol and hide my face under my pillow until the darkness takes my headache and I finally fall asleep.

The alibi is good. Tiffani Cane is clear. Thanks to her rocky marriage, her cancelled coffee date, her busy attorney who couldn't do it any other time. She was there that morning in his office, for two hours—the hours of the day Phil and Melanie wound up dead.

Which means that the case, well, it's back to square one. Anderson isn't happy about it. Neither is the chief. It's a case that's gone cold, a case with no more leads, a case that is over two weeks old.

Sal arrives with roses for the gala. All I can think is that I wish we were driving separately. "Wow, Macie," he says when he see me. "Just wow."

I've done it. Silver dress. Even the lipstick. I've spent most of my life with naked lips, occasionally donning something neutral and unnoticeable for a big event like a wedding. I feel like some type of peacock now, standing in front of him. The interesting thing is that I didn't feel like a peacock before he arrived. I actually felt kind of…pretty. The silver and the red—they looked good together. In fact, I even sprang for a pair of red heels to match my face. As in, I just bought shoes to match my lip color. This is new ground for me, and now that Sal is standing there—fitted suit, shiny black shoes, and a red and silver tie to match me, well, I feel...confused. He's beautiful, no doubt, but I know that I look at him like I might a piece of art, a really nice guy piece of art, but not really a life companion. And, why?

Who knows, but as all these thoughts are plowing along through my brain, I'm chatting away with Sal about work and the weather and the roses. I'm cutting off the bottoms of the stems and finding a vase (do I have a vase? Yup, one right here at the back of my cupboard), and offering him a drink, which he turns down, and I'm relieved, I think.

And then we're in his car, and it's freshly vacuumed and smells nice; he does too. And I feel like I'm on a date to the prom, which I basically am, except with more legal alcohol, and I feel the same twittery nervousness I might have at age sixteen, but with more womanly jadedness, and something else—a feeling that something is a little wobbly. Even though things look right. We look right—he and I. I could see it the moment he opened the door. He's big enough to make me small. I could tuck right into those huge shoulders, that lovely chest. And with his black and my silver and the red, well, we just kind of popped. One of those photographs that are mostly black and white with only one bright color. But no matter how right we look, something's off, like a puzzle piece you're trying to shove into the right spot because it's…just… almost…perfect.

The gala—it's not like the movies—in case you were wondering, in case the only reference you have for a word like *gala* is this tuxedoed event that Bruce Wayne is attending with clinking glasses and a string quartet playing in the background. No, this is much more sinister than Batman. There's a really loud DJ playing really loud music even though very few people are dancing. And all around at tables and the bar are a bunch of people much too old to feel uninhibited without the use of loads of booze. And booze, my friends, is flowing. I mean, we're not to bowties-askew-and-lipstick-smudged zone yet, but we'll get there much more quickly than I originally thought. Fortunately, there's a bit of food first. I order a lemon-glazed tilapia and pasta while Sal has gone for the sirloin with potatoes option. Both of us picked asparagus. We have to lean close together to hear each other over the music and that obnoxious DJ, and so we tip our heads together over the table, like two perfect lovers, talking about how the food tastes (his isn't bad; mine's a bit fishy and a bit cold, but there's pasta and lemon, so we'll let bygones be bygones). He has a glass of wine, loosens his tie, chats about the work he's been doing this week.

Turns down a second glass of wine and asks me about my case.

"Case?" I say.

"Sure," he answers. "The murder-suicide."

"I mean, it's really Anderson's case. I'm just there to be some extra ears and eyes."

"Yeah, sure, and Tad's crazy good at that stuff. At least the ears stuff." And then he looks at me like something has just occurred to him. "You that good?"

I don't answer. Instead, I do a switch that I wonder if Sal will notice. "Is Tad really that good? What other cases has he solved?"

Sal smiles and I think I'm caught, but then he answers, "Well, like you say, they're not really his cases, but he works a lot with Anderson, sometimes with Brandt. Anderson can talk all the crap he wants, but Tad has given him important evidence about homicides at least a dozen times. And the dude can't even see."

"Technically, he can," I say. "See, I mean."

"Right, okay," Sal says, "but, you know what I mean."

"Yeah, right," I add, because of course I know what he means. I just… who knows what I'm playing at here?

"Tad's helped with a bunch of other cases too—

smaller things, like missing persons and abuse cases and stuff like that." Sal squints at me over his remaining asparagus.

"So tell me, Macie. Why'd they bring you on? If Tad's that good."

I shrug. "I can draw, I guess."

"Lots of people can draw."

I shrug again.

"You remember," he says, and when he does it almost sounds accusatory. "You have a photographic memory."

"With some things," I say, spearing a bit of cold fish.

"Tad has that too, but it's more with sounds and sensory stuff. You're like the Tad with eyes."

"I guess," I say.

He looks at me, unsatisfied. "You guess?"

"I'm good at it," I confess.

"If they put you with Tad and Anderson, then you're better than good."

I push around a piece of pasta, not sure why the thing that should be a compliment feels more like an unveiling. I finish my meat, take a swig of my drink, wash it down with plain water. "Anderson doesn't love having me around, either of us honestly, but especially me."

"Oh, he loves it," Sal answers. "Otherwise, he wouldn't have it."

A waiter comes by and I push my plate in his direction.

"Want to dance?" Sal asks.

"I'm not good."

"Hmph," Sal says. "You were great at line dancing."

"You were just tipsy enough that I looked great," I reply, smiling.

He glances sideways at me. "You saying I should have another drink?"

"I mean, it depends on how much you value your toes."

He wiggles his shoes and laughs. "I think I can take it. We'll just do a slow one that doesn't require any big moves."

Great. Then, like he's cued it, a soft ballad comes on. He takes my hand and leads me to the floor where a sum total of maybe three other couples are dancing, though several couples are at the bar building up their liquid courage. Sal pulls me in, swaying softly. He tucks his arm fully around my back, all the way to my other ribs. I sway with his sway and it's definitely easy. He has a good sense of rhythm, a nice body to sink into. I don't actually step on his toes; we'd need something more complex to merit that. He tucks his head onto my head, wrapping me up and I admit that I kind of lean into it, just as Tad walks in. Tux fitted in a perfect V along his shoulders and waist. The waves of his hair running along his temples. Eyes blue as ice. And the most perfect redhead you've ever seen at his side. I mean, we're talking ginger goldilocks. That hair's not from a bottle either. It falls in waves, just like his, only all the way down to her waist. She's wearing a red dress, the type that sashays back and forth across her body, and she totally owns every inch of it. Subconsciously I rub my lips together, wishing I had a napkin to wipe the stupid lipstick off of my face. And then she turns, and it's Rebecca, the temp receptionist, the redhead who said I should make a play for Sal, the redhead who showed up at work the next Monday, the redhead half the office has been swooning over. She puts a hand on Tad's wrist and they turn toward their table. It's then that I step on one of Sal's toes.

He pulls me back just a few inches, looks into my eyes, and then belly laughs. "You got me," he says.

"Wasn't even a difficult song," I reply. The song, mercifully, finishes at that moment. "I need a cheese-cake," I say.

"Well, I do what the lady says," Sal responds.

A large dessert bar runs along the far wall of the

banquet hall. They've got a series of cakes, plates of fruits, a chocolate fountain, and enough cheesecake to feed Mongolia. I've got no appetite, but I need to sit and put something in my mouth.

Sal chooses a chocolate. I go for the mango lime.

"Think these are house made?" he asks.

"I'd bet the farm that they're shipped in frozen from somewhere boringly generic."

"Cheesecake factory?"

"We can only hope," I say.

For reasons no sane individual could fathom, I position myself at our table in a place where I can see Tad and Rebecca talking.

She laughs a lot and orders white wine with her fish. It's probably the perfect pairing, for people who know how to pair things.

I shove a bite of cheesecake into my face just as Sal asks what job I did before here. That innocent question catches me off guard and my face flushes. "A dentist's office," I stammer.

"You were a dentist?" he asks, a small wrinkle of confusion between his eyebrows.

"No, I worked at the office," I say. "Just a receptionist."

"From there to here," he says. "Big shift."

"You have no idea."

"You leave because you were bored?"

And I guess to a cop that would make sense. Why would anyone spend the day filing paperwork about insurance information and cavities and family histories when they could be researching crimes and apprehending bad guys.

"Not really bored," I say. "Just needed a change."

He gives me a knowing nod. "Your husband still work there? Your ex?"

"Oh," I say with surprise. "No. He doesn't really work anywhere. He wanders. And I don't. I guess I was too boring for him."

"You?" Sal says.

"Shocking as it may seem that the woman who worked as a dental receptionist and faithfully balances her online checkbook might be boring, but yeah, that's why. He wanted to see the world, find nirvana, something."

"He succeed?"

I smile at the question. "I don't know, but I'm guessing he's probably just mired in credit card debt."

"Kids?" Sal asks. "Did he want them?"

"I don't think so," I say. "We never got far enough to hash that one out."

"How's your cheesecake?" he asks, tactfully changing the subject, and I swear he's the absolute nicest human in the whole world.

"It's a solid B+."

"Mine's not bad either. Another dance?"

It's something fast this time and I hesitate, but Sal grabs my hand and pulls me to the dance floor. Others are loosening up too, bopping and occasionally grinding their way along the dance floor. I sway awkwardly like a teen. He takes my hand, twirls me around a time or two, does something that looks like a swing type move, or at least a something type move. Neither of us is amazing, but we're dancing and that's what we're supposed to do, right? Because it's fun, right? I catch a glimpse of Tad, tapping away on the table. His date is talking and in that quick glance I can't tell if he's tapping to the music or to the rhythm of her story. She steals a glance toward the dance floor and for a second our eyes meet in this funny way. And I know she wants to be here, dancing. And I know suddenly that I don't. When the song ends, a slow one begins and Sal has me wrapped up before I can stop him. Rebecca is pulling Tad to the floor, and he's tapping his way through the crowd with his feet—no cane. I can tell it makes him move more carefully, slowly, but he's found the music. I haven't. I bump Sal's toe with one of mine and he grins, pulling me in tighter. I'm starting to feel hot, overheated if I'm being honest, when that obnoxious DJ gets on and says it's time to switch it up and everybody grab a new partner. I cling to Sal's hand, not at all wanting a new partner, when a soft, long finger taps my shoulder. Sal grins, letting me go, and I find myself face to face with Tad. "Hey," I say, glad that I've been moving so the flush of my cheeks doesn't look obvious. Sal has gathered Rebecca up into that chest of his and she looks like she could think of a worse fate.

"So you asked her out?" I ask, nodding to his date, before any modicum of filter kicks into my brain.

He laughs. "You suggested it. And—funny story—you're never going to believe this."

"I wouldn't know," I say. "Unless you tell it."

"Remember my friend from high school—the one with the duck and the YouTube channel."

"Yes…" I say cautiously.

"That's her little sister. I didn't even recognize her. Last I saw her, she was in pigtails."

"Well, she's not anymore."

"Nope."

"So, how'd you find out?" I ask. "More detectiving."

"We're not detectives," he says without skipping a beat, and I see the soft smile. "We figured it out at lunch one day. She came out to the courtyard, kind of hiding from one of the guys. We got to talking, and put two and two together."

"Two and two, huh?" I say. Wishing that was something I could do. With the case. With my personal life. With anything at all, really.

"Don't make it sound so sinister, Macie."

But I didn't, did I?

For a few seconds, we just sway, in perfect sync.

"You're not a bad dancer," I say, changing the subject.

"Surprised?" he asks.

Am I? I mean, he's tapping to some kind of rhythm nearly every minute of the day, but somehow that never seemed like it would apply to music before. "A little."

"I like to dance," he says. "I mean, you won't catch me on a swing floor, but a little slow dance, I can handle that. It's about sound and movement, not sight. Look around. I bet half these people have their eyes closed anyway."

And they did. Women leaning on chests or shoulders. Men holding waists and kissing hair. A surprising number of closed eyes. Not mine. They'd been wide open the whole night.

"Plus," Tad says. "When people are forced to be this close to me, I can see into their faces without looking like a nut job." He smiles, looking straight into my eyes. I take a step closer to him, not even realizing I'm doing it.

"Can you see my whole face?" I ask, because I guess I'm just rude like that.

"Can you see through a pinhole?" he asks. "Go on. Make one with your fist and look at me."

I do. I don't see all of him, but I do see quite a bit. The blue eyes, the sharp cheeks, soft lips. I let my hand slip down and I feel things too—the sinewy shoulder under my hand, the soft rounding of his chest, the sharp lines of muscle along his arms. I've leaned another step in, my mouth just below his. His nose touches mine for a moment, a flash, and I open my lips like someone else just took over my very practical body. Then I see Sal glance at us and I jerk back. I'm breathing like I've just run a lap. Where is that stupid DJ? He should be telling us to switch up the partners again.

"Did I get your foot?" Tad asks.

I know he knows he didn't—Tad would feel something like that, and he's just staring at me and I'm not used to it, and his eyes, and his lips. Now I can't breathe at all. The song ends, but my brain doesn't catch up with that so I sway a few more steps, my face now a solid six inches from Tad—a nice respectable distance. Sal is walking Tad's date back to the table, and I'm fully flushed now.

"I'm not feeling great," I blurt out and rush to the lady's room.

When I get there and look at my face, it's red—deep, solid almost-purple-red, red enough to match my lips, all the way up to my hairline like a beet.

"Hey, you okay?" Rebecca pops her head in. "Tad asked me to see if you were okay."

"Oh, yeah," I say, wiping my forehead. "Just got a little hot in there. I'm kind of just an…"

"…introvert," she says, finishing the sentence in a way I wasn't going to. "Yeah, me too."

And I don't know what it is, but somehow I didn't realize they made introverts in double D cup sizes. I clear my throat.

"When they made us switch partners, I thought I was going to die. Of course it could have been worse." She winks, handing me a wet towel, and I wipe my forehead absently.

"Great lipstick by the way," she says.

"My friend sells it," I say, before I can think to stop myself.

"Cool."

And then we stare at each other awkwardly. Like introverts do.

"Maybe I can get you her number or something. If you're interested. I mean, in lipstick. Here, let me just text it to you."

"Sure," she says, giving me her number.

"You know," I say, just jumping in. "I think I was a little rude the first time we met."

"Well, I was nearly hitting on your date," she answers.

"No," I say, pausing, thinking, still wiping the sweat off my face. "You weren't. You were asking me why *I* wasn't hitting on my date."

She doesn't say anything, just lets the words hang in the air.

And then, with that little sashay as she moves toward the door, she says, "And why weren't you? Aren't you?"

"Look, thanks for checking on me. You can tell Sal…" I pause, look at myself in the mirror. I'm still purple. "Actually, I think I'll just get an Uber home. Tell him that, will you?"

"Sure," Rebecca says, though I can tell she feels doubtful about it. "But are you sure you don't want to go tell him yourself. I mean…"

"No, I don't want to inconvenience him and I might throw up or something, so I'll just…"

"…get an Uber," she finishes, and I hear how bad it will sound, but I'm already shooting forward, throwing the damp towel away, gripping my purse, fleeing from the bathroom, from Tad's date, and from something else that feels a whole lot like myself.

By the time I plunk into the Uber, I've got two messages from Sal. "Why'd you leave? Are you okay?" Along with a message from my ex—that one I delete without reading.

Turns out I should have read it, because when I flip on the light to my living room, a nearly naked man is asleep under my throw blanket.

I scream.

He rolls over.

"What the—" I yell.

"Geez, Macie, calm down," Alex says, scratching at some unmentionable place beneath the blanket. "I needed a place to crash for the night."

"How did you even get in?"

He rolls his eyes. Man, I forgot how much I hated that.

"You always hide the key in the same place, Macie."

You're too boring, Macie. That's what I hear in in his voice.

"Noted," I say.

He shrugs like it will be there the next time. Also, like he's never heard of a hotel before. Or boundaries of any kind.

Maybe I haven't either, because I don't kick him out right that second. I'm trying to decide if I should call a car for him or make him do it himself, or maybe just let him stay there. It's already after nine and I just want to roll into my own bed, not deal with getting an unwanted man out of my house.

Of course I'll have to get him out sometime. And then the doorbell rings.

Alex legit puts the pillow over his head.

I open the door—not quite sure what I was thinking there—just childhood conditioning, and Sal is standing on my porch looking a little concerned and a little…miffed.

"Oh, hey." I cough, like I'm in a B movie. "I'm sorry I left. I started to feel a little sick, didn't want you to have to drive me home and risk getting sick yourself."

"So you cared about my health, but not the Uber guy's health."

"I—"

Alex chooses that moment to let out a king fart.

"Is someone in here?" Sal asks.

I step aside. If he wants to be in a room with Alex's gas, then I guess that's his prerogative. Sal sees the lump of man on my couch, and I'm not quite sure what I'm thinking—something about how obvious it must be that my deadbeat of an ex came and crashed here. Turns out, Sal is not thinking that at all.

"You invited a man over?" he asks, the hurt and anger mingling in his voice. He faces the couch the same way it seems he must face down criminals—legs wide, shoulders back, ready to spring. Alex moans.

"Oh, no," I say quickly. "I didn't invite him over."

"So he just found his way here?" Sal turns to me. Or maybe he turns on me; it's unclear. We step back toward the front entryway, whispering to each other. "I guess that's what you were rushing home to," he says.

I'm pretty sure it's the least true thing he's ever said. "Whoa, no. He's my ex," I stutter.

"Got it," Sal says. "Old flame."

"No flame."

"He's naked on your couch, Macie."

This doesn't seem like the right moment to point out that he usually wears briefs when he sleeps.

"You just had to say there was someone else," Sal says.

"There isn't," I plead.

"Obviously, there is."

"No," I insist, my voice edging toward a whimper —the same voice I used when Alex was leaving me. But why, when I've been happier since he left, when I'm really unhappy that he's back. Why whimper to Sal, or plead either? After all, this is my house, and I get to choose who sleeps on my couch, and also who I date. My voice gets stronger, just a little.

"There isn't anything going on with that stinky, half-asleep man on my couch," I repeat. "There was barely anything going on when we were married."

Sal looks somewhat pacified, until I keep talking, because now I can't stop. "But, Sal, this thing between us isn't going to work either. I don't know why. You're—" I gesture at the muscles pressing against the suit, "—gorgeous. And sweet. And just a really great guy. But look at my life—" I wave my hand back at my ex. "Maybe I need someone more broken. Or someone, at least, who understands broken."

"That's the stupidest thing I ever heard, Macie."

"Look, Sal, maybe this isn't a good…"

"..This isn't a good time?" he finishes for me.

I purse my lips. "This isn't a good *fit*. If you're this mad that my bum of an ex plopped his half-naked self on my couch without permission. If you can't even laugh at the absurdity of that, then I don't really think it'll work."

"I can laugh," he says with the most stoic face I've ever seen.

I cross my arms.

"Just not right now."

"Right," I say. "Because you're way too functional for this kind of nutsy."

"You're not nutsy," he says as though he wasn't just accusing me of cheating on him with my ex-husband.

"I mean, I'm a little nutsy."

He glances through the dim light at Alex, who's begun snoring. Oh man, I do NOT miss that.

"Macie," Sal says, stepping inside. "I can handle a little nutsy, I mean, not full-blown—like he's not moving in or something, right?"

"No," I say. "I'm calling an Uber as soon as you leave."

"Right. Good," he says. "But that's not really the thing. This guy. That's not why you left the gala."

"Definitely not," I say.

"But you're clearly not sick."

I reach up and touch my cheeks like I'm back in that bathroom. "I really didn't feel well," I say.

"Maybe not, but let's at least be honest with each other. Really honest. It's not that we won't work because we can't; we won't work because you don't really want us to."

I stare at him, not knowing what to say because he has hit the nail so perfectly on the head. He must see it in my eyes because he leans down and kisses my head. "It's okay," he says. "I should have seen it at the first."

Seen what?

"But go on and call that Uber now because if that guy doesn't leave you'll have to call the cops anyway. Might as well do it while I'm still here."

I grin. "Hey, Sleeping Beauty." I walk in and jostle Alex's shoulder. "I'm calling an Uber."

"You kidding me, Macie?" he says. "It's just one night."

"Nope," I say. "You can get a hotel."

"I don't have cash for a hotel."

"Turns out they also take cards. But if you don't have one of those, a hostel, then. You like hostels."

He's sitting up now, staring at Sal, who's leaning against the door frame—a big hulking man in black.

"My date," I say just as Sal introduces himself, "Police."

"Both," I clarify. "Now go. I'll pay for the Uber. Where do you want it to take you?"

"The men's shelter, I guess."

I level my gaze at him, like a mother. Ugh, no wonder we didn't work out.

"Fine," he says. "The Sheraton."

Sal pops an eyebrow. He sees what I see—the Sheraton's not bad for a man with no money.

When Alex is dressed in his tunic and on his way to a solidly mid-level hotel, I turn to Sal. "You ready to laugh yet?"

"Yeah, kinda," he says.

And we both laugh.

"You want a cup of coffee?" I ask.

"Nah," he says. "I should probably be on my way. Thanks for the entertainment, Macie."

"Yeah, well, I guess it's what I do."

"Keep doing it." He kisses my head again and is gone in a swish of fitted black tux—like Bruce Wayne and Batman merged for the night. I hope I didn't make a mistake sending him away. Though—perfect shoulders aside—I know I haven't. What he said was true. It's not that we couldn't have fit. It's that I didn't want to. Though there is still that little pesky question rattling around in my brain. *Why?*

———

I fix myself a chamomile tea so I can settle down, and look for something boring to listen to. The drive with the recordings is on my desk. I put it into my laptop, and set it to play. The same messages I've heard from the water company, insurance scams, and maybe one call that isn't a scam—doesn't matter to the Samuelsons now I guess. Several messages from the renter with the raccoon in her shed. One from a friend inviting them for drinks; one from a lady at their church about helping with soup kitchen. I wonder for the millionth time why these people are dead when so many jerks seem to live forever. Then another message from the little old lady renting the house. The critter is still in the shed; she's disappointed they haven't called back; she's thinking of calling pest control herself; and then another one asking them to call pest control. Her dog barks every time the answering machine picks up. And I sure hope the executor of the estate has caught up with her because it's going to be a shock when she finds out that her landlords were brutally murdered.

I stop mid-thought. Rewind the recording and listen to the dog again. Every time the machine picks up.

Thousands of renters have dogs, and I'm pretty sure this elderly woman didn't murder the couple and then leave eighteen messages about a raccoon in the shed. But I text Tad anyway, even though it's late and he was on a date.

He doesn't reply till I've almost fallen asleep. "I'm tired, Macie. Let's talk in the morning."

Sure, whatever. I drag from my couch to my bed.

"Sal gone?" he texts as I'm settling into the covers.

"Yeah," I say.

hen I click off my alarm, I see that Alex has left three messages about how badly he slept. I erase them all.

And then I realize it's Saturday. I head to the station to meet Tad anyway. It's pouring buckets and no one's there except Officer Long, pounding through some paperwork. When Tad finally shows up (okay, he's only five minutes late), he's nursing a coffee and looking rumpled. I guess he had fun last night. It's not a thought that makes me happy.

"What's up?" he asks, taking a swig of his coffee.

"Well, I was re-listening to the messages last night."

"With Sal there?" he interrupts.

"No, Sal had left, a long time before that."

"How late were you up?"

"Sal left early," I say.

He gives me a look.

"We, um, we broke up."

"Really?" he asks. "Why?"

"It just wasn't right," I answer. "Look, can we stay on topic?"

He holds up a hand in surrender.

"So I was listening to the messages…"

"And you decoded something?" He gives me a half smile.

"There's a dog," I say in a rush. "Every time the renter calls, this dog barks."

He looks at me, kind of flat and tired.

"Every time," I say, trying to make something that seems lame sound more interesting. "Every time the machine picks up it barks."

"Macie," he says like he can't believe he's in the office on a Saturday. "People have dogs, especially renters. And they bark."

"It just felt…" I fish for something. "Really regular."

He runs a hand through the waves of his hair, holds out a hand. "Give it to me," he says. "I'll have a listen."

"I was thinking I would talk to Anderson about it too."

"Maybe better have me listen first."

"I mean, why not interview the renter also," I say, ignoring him.

"Anderson's gonna say 'no,'" Tad answers.

"Why do you think so?" I ask. It's a dumb question, one that Tad doesn't grace with an answer.

I slump into the seat across from him.

"Also," he says, looking up from his coffee. "Anderson's closing the case as soon as he can. He said so last night. He says we just don't have any evidence, nothing to go on."

I rub my forehead. "Just will you listen to the messages again?"

"Sure, Macie. But we both know what I'm going to hear. A dog. Barking."

He's right about Anderson. When I text him about visiting the old woman he shuts the idea down before I can even make an argument for the idea. "We're not harassing more people. The case is closing. Monday morning if I can swing it."

That leaves time for one more drive along my old haunts—the house, a fat For Sale sign dug into the lawn. The gray skies, the pouring rain. It makes everything seem that much sadder. After that, I drive past each other house (well, mansion) we visited and finally wind up at the one place I've gone several times since this all began—the humane society.

When I walk in, my jacket dripping from the rain, John greets me. "Any newbies?" I ask.

His eyes twinkle. "A litter of kittens today," he says. "Cutest things you've ever seen. Come on, you look sad. I'll let you hold one—that'll cheer you up."

"I really don't have time today," I start to say.

"Everyone's got time for kittens," he says, unlocking the door to the cat room before I can argue further.

And, I mean, John's been wrong before, but these are the cutest things I've ever seen. Little balls of somersaulting fluff. He must see it on my face because he says, "Told you," as he unlocks the cage. "These kiddos will be gone in a flash once they're weaned."

An orange one tumbles into my palm and blinks up at me before stretching and padding at my arm. "I didn't even know they got this fluffy. They're like—" But I'm interrupted by a ringing of the door.

"Excuse me," John says and I have to admit I'm happy to settle in with the little orange, who's now burrowing against my sweater. John's left the cage unlocked and the others come out as well and are making their way to the warmth that is my lap while a naughty one chases a spider in the corner.

I hear it then. A voice ringed with tears, but still distinct.

"Okay, slow down," John is saying. "Did you have the animal registered?"

I lean in to hear the voice again, try to place it. The orange cat is kind of sucking at one of my knuckles.

"I can't believe my dog ran off like that," she's saying. "My son brought him two weeks ago. We've been getting on so well. This morning I let him out to do his business in the rain and he chewed through the leash." She's crying again.

"Is he registered?" John asks again and then I find it—the voice. She's the woman from the messages, the renter. I shuffle with my lap of cats closer to the door.

"I didn't know I had to register a dog," she's saying.

"Now don't you worry," John's cooing. "Let's have a look around. Haven't gotten any new dogs today, but..."

"He ran away today," she says.

"Okay, let's start with his name, and then get a good description. I'll call you if someone brings him in."

She sniffles and I desperately try to shuffle the cats back into their cage. It's a little like, well, herding cats.

The orange one clings to my sweater with tiny needles of claw. The one in the corner has spider web all over its whiskers. "You guys," I mutter, lifting the two sleepy ones in. The woman's description—I strain to hear it since she's whisper-crying now. I disentangle Orange and then manage to capture the spider hunter, just as John comes back.

"Poor woman," he clucks, locking up the cage and turning to me. "Did a little kitten therapy help?"

"You know, John," I say, digging out my keys. "It really, really did."

He beams. "They'll be weaned by next week. You have one you want me to hold?" I glance at the orange, then at the spider hunter.

"I've got to get back to you," I say, waving my cell phone and hustling out.

Once in my car I call Tad. "You're not going to believe this," I say.

"You know," he says. "I was just about to say the same thing to you."

CHAPTER 31

"So?" I ask when Tad sinks into the passenger's seat, even though it takes every ounce of restraint I have not to blurt out my own news.

"So you were right," he says. "A dog barks. Every time."

"Are you teasing me?" I ask.

"A little," he answers. "But not really. Because it's more than just a dog barking during a phone call, even more than the dog barking with regularity during a phone call. That dog barked at the exact instant when it would have heard the name and voice on the answering machine. It didn't bark when the old lady said, 'Hello.' It didn't bark when she started to speak. In fact, it didn't bark at all during the rest of the conversation at all. It only barked as the answering machine picked up. Like it was barking to the voice on the other line."

I nod.

"Which could be a total coincidence, Macie—prepare yourself for that. Maybe it barks every time it hears someone's voice on the phone no matter what, maybe it barks when it sees its owner pick up a phone, maybe that's just an obnoxious thing it does. But it really did sound like the dog was responding to the caller's voice. In this case, it would have been the recorded voice of Phil Samuelson."

"Speaking of voices," I say. "I stopped by the humane society today."

"Okay," he says. "Not a bad idea, but Anderson called two weeks ago."

"I know. I stopped by then too. In fact, I've stopped by several times in the last little while. But this time I heard something."

"An evil plot to steal a dog?"

"No," I say. "No mob bosses came in either. Unfortunately. But someone came in while I was holding these really cute kittens."

"Kittens?" he asks.

"That's not the point," I say. "A woman came in all worked up about her dog running away, just this morning."

"That sounds like the humane society," he says.

"But it wasn't just any woman," I answer. "It was *the* woman. The renter. And she's only had the dog for a few weeks and this morning it chewed through its leash and ran off."

I risk a quick glance in his direction.

"I take it the humane society didn't have the dog."

"None at all have come in today."

"So where are we driving?" Tad asks, though I think he knows.

I hang a now-familiar right into a now familiar neighborhood. He presses his face against the glass, though I doubt he can see too much through the rivers of rain.

We pull up in front of the house, in front of the For Sale sign.

The rain is thundering down now, like it's nailing holes into my car. Tad and I sit for a long moment before he pulls at the handle and opens the door, tapping his way over the curb with his cane.

I slip the hood of my jacket tight over my head. The front of the house looks as it normally does, but Tad and I both hear the sound from the back, the shuffle then a whine.

We walk around to the back stoop. And there he is, our only witness, looking wet and sad. And none too happy to see the two of us.

"Hey, boy," I coo, as the dog begins to growl.

Tad takes my arm and we both back up slightly, wondering if the dog is going to attack. He's not a small dog, not a lap poodle, but a full grown one, who hasn't had his hair cut in weeks, which makes him look bigger and less froufrou.

He doesn't charge. In fact, as we back away, he seems to as well, standing guard at the back door, making himself as big and menacing as possible. It's maybe the saddest thing I've ever seen.

Tad's on his phone. "Anderson," I hear him saying. "We found you a witness."

I hear Anderson swear even with the rain. Tad moves the phone away from his ear.

"He'll be here in ten," Tad says.

"Should we wait in the car?" I ask, though I can see the rain dripping from Tad's hair to his shoulders down his back; and I know I'm no better. The water has soaked through my jacket to my shirt and all the way to my skin.

"Only if you want to ruin your car or the both of us strip down."

I swallow at the suggestion. "Maybe the front porch."

We back away from the dog who is still growling and I make a phone call of my own. "Hey, John," I say. "We've found a lost dog. Can you come help get it?"

"We?" John asks.

"My partner and I," I say.

"Oh, Macie, I didn't realize you were with some-one. You should have brought him in to choose an animal."

He assumed I was lonely—is it that obvious? "Um, no, I mean my work partner. Anyway, here's the address, and John, you might see some cop cars. Don't let it freak you out."

<hr>

John doesn't see any cop cars. Because he arrives before Anderson. I don't know why that's so annoying to me. I mean, it's for the best. Cops will shoot a threatening animal without a second thought, even if it is their only witness. But is Anderson not taking this seriously at all? The dog is alive. He was with a woman who was renting the house from them. The implications are huge.

"It's the poodle," John says, opening a cage and retrieving a few tools from his van. "Does it seem violent?" he asks us, sitting dripping on the porch.

"A little protective of this house, maybe," I say.

John gives me a confused look.

"It's a really long story," I say.

"I'll just call the owner," he says, opening a little notebook he has.

"Nope," I say. "You can't."

He gives me a more confused look.

"She might not be the owner," I reply. "It's a really long story. I'll let the police explain when they get here. *If* they get here."

Which they don't. When Tad calls Anderson back, Anderson is grim and frantic. One of their officers was shot in a routine traffic stop. The shooter is gone; he just drove off. And their guy is in critical condition. They don't have time for a dog right now.

"Who got shot?" Tad asks.

I lean close to listen. Not the name of a person I know, but Tad covers his mouth when he hears it.

"I'm so sorry," I say when he hangs up the phone. "Did you know him well?"

He shakes his head. "Not well, but we knew each other." He clears his throat, tries to straighten his shoulders, but they slump anyway. I pat him awkwardly on the arm while John looks on.

"What is going on?" John asks. "You know, I can just call the owner. I think it would be the easiest thing."

I shake my head. "She might not be the actual owner. I mean, maybe she is now. But originally, we believe these people were the owners." I gesture to the house.

"No one else has called me for a missing poodle," he interrupts. "And these breeds are popular."

"They wouldn't have been in a state to call," I say. "They were killed a few weeks ago and the case is under investigation and you're probably not supposed to know any of this at all, but John, I need you to take the dog in and not call that woman and not let her know if she calls you."

John gapes at me. Like, his mouth literally opens.

"Please," I say.

"Are you a police officer?" he asks.

"Not exactly. I'm…" Who am I? No one really. Barely more than a citizen. "I have a photographic memory, especially for certain things, so I help with some of the cases. Tad too." I wave toward Tad, who is looking ashen and tapping his cane anxiously.

John casts a suspicious glance at the cane, probably wondering how a blind guy helps the police.

"Please," I say again, "As a favor to me."

"Macie," he says. "If this is a stunt of some type or because you want that dog or something."

"I don't want this dog," I say and it's the truest thing I've ever said. The story is too sad and I'm too stuck in it. "Please."

He takes a leash muzzle thing, plus a treat for bait and goes out back.

Within minutes, he has Bernard in a cage and I swear the dog is crying.

"Macie," John warns, rain dripping from his hood to his forehead. "Do you really want me to kennel this poor dog?"

"When you get back to your office," I say, "check him for registration, or whatever it was you were asking that lady for. Most dogs have chips, right?"

"She didn't register him."

"I know," I say. "But I'm betting someone did. I'm betting the address matches this house right here, not the one she gave you. Just check it."

"And if it does?" he asks.

"Call me," I say. "Also, I think the dog will answer to Bernard." Sure enough, the dog's ears perk slightly at the name. "Take good care of him, John. He's had a rough month."

"I always take good care of them," John says. "But a kennel's a kennel, and he's not going to like it."

"What dog does?" I ask, feeling like the rain has leaked inside of me.

He nods and closes the van door. I can still hear Bernard whimpering. Tad, on the other hand, is completely silent.

"Come on," I say. "I'll take you home so you can

change. Then we can go to the hospital to see your cop friend."

Tad shakes his head. "They're not letting anyone but family in. Take me home; get some clothes yourself, then let's go to that rental house."

"Are you kidding?"

"What else are we going to do, Macie? We found the dog, and the person who had it. Anderson's not in a place to do anything about it right now. So, come on." I realize he's walked off the porch and is standing in the rain, waiting for me.

CHAPTER 32

When I get back to Tad's house to pick him up for the second time today, he's holding a coffee for me. "I added some chocolate to it. It's a warm drinks kind of day."

"Thank you," I say. "I'm so sorry about your friend."

"He was more of an associate; I didn't know him really well. But I'm still just really—I don't even know the word—shocked, sad, something. He had a wife."

I think about Rachel and Aiden, find myself nearly choking up over the cop I don't know.

"Hopefully he'll be okay," Tad says. "But the timing sure sucks."

I nod, taking a sip of my drink, which is definitely more chocolate than coffee, and that's definitely the way I would have chosen for it to be. How did Tad know?

"Are you worried?" Tad asks as I drive to an older part of town—the houses squat and sinking, though several still host pots, empty and waiting for the flower of spring.

"She's just an old woman," I reply.

"With a stolen dog."

"I don't think she's the one who stole it."

"Right," Tad says. "That's exactly the part that worries me."

The rain has slowed by the time we arrive and I knock on the door. The old woman peeps through the opening—just one little sliver of her gray eye showing.

"Hello," I say.

"Who are you?" she grumps.

I notice the 'Beware of Dog' signs posted on the pole by the carport.

"I, uh…" Tad is standing behind me and in that flash I realize I have no badge, no search warrant, no credentials, no nothing. I'm wearing a freaking cardigan. "I got a call about a pest problem you were having."

"Oh, thank heavens," she says, opening the door without another thought, not even considering the cardigan.

She's a tiny woman, probably barely grazing five feet. Gray hair, gray eyes, leathery skin. Bland clothes, but neat and clean. Her house smells lightly of age and strongly of lemon. There's a little bit of wet dog under both of those and something else sour and stale.

I clear my throat as Tad taps his way over the doorstep. "Now, where was the problem?"

"I've been calling for weeks," she says, not answering the question. "I thought when my son brought me a dog that it would…" and then she tears up.

"Excuse me," I say.

"Sorry," she says. "My dog ran off this morning."

"How awful," I reply.

"He was a beautiful dog," she says, "and I was just sure that once I got him the critter in my shed would go away, but I still hear it, always at night. Though Harry used to growl at it, through the wall."

"Harry?" I ask.

"My dog." She leads us through the house, and I have no way to communicate with Tad about anything, but I hear him moving slowly behind me.

"It's always right here," she says, pointing to a

wall in the kitchen. I think it's stuck in the shed or something. But every morning when I go out to check, nothing's there."

The shed is connected to the kitchen, in that weird way old houses are sometimes stuck together. Like some old guy got bored twenty years ago, decided he needed a shed, and tacked it on to the house.

"Have you noticed any droppings?" I ask, at a loss for what else to say.

"No," she replies, "but like I said, I think the animal is stuck somewhere. At this point I'm just waiting for it to die, and then it'll rot and smell."

"Yes," I say. "We wouldn't want that to happen."

"So how do you get it out?" she asks. "It's been weeks. I've been calling and calling."

"Can we have a look in the shed, ma'am?" Tad says, and I can't believe he's going along with this.

"Sure," she says. "That's what Mr. Samuelson— you know, the landlord—did last time he came out. But that was almost three weeks ago. He didn't seem too happy about the shed when he came out, but then he never took care of it."

"Is he usually a neglectful landlord?" I ask.

"Well, no," she said. "Not usually. So I'm worried it's something expensive—to ignore me like that."

She takes a small key from beside the door and

undoes the padlock on the shed. It's spacious in there, and only has a few very normal things sitting around—an old lawnmower I can't imagine her using, several pairs of moldy garden gloves, a couple of rusted hedge clippers, a rake, and a few gray packets of seeds.

"I take it you don't come out here much," Tad says and I can hear him breathing, the deep inhales. I breathe with him, trying to find what he finds.

"Not if I can help it," she says. "My son does the lawn in the summer. I pay him a little. And my gardening days are long past. Perfect for some critter to come on in and make a home."

"It really is," Tad says, tapping along the wall. "You *see* anything, Macie?" he asks. "Any *droppings* or anything?"

And I mean, I never said I was brilliant, but I can tell Tad is hinting at something and I start to look around. I notice the faint scent of cigarette, which is odd considering her house smelled as disinfected as a hospital, or at least a nursing home. And on the floor, sure enough, I notice a little ring of ash—like someone had an ashtray in here and then took it out. "Hmm," I say, sounding like maybe the worst actor ever, but this lady doesn't seem to notice. "This might be something. I remove my phone and snap a picture, adding, "It's honestly much cleaner in here than I thought it'd be with a pest." And then I notice how truly clean it is—this shed that's barely been used for months. Aside from the ash ring, there's no dust or dirt on the shelves or floor, no old dead leaves, like it's been recently and regularly and thoroughly swept.

"He's in the wall," she says with exasperation. "That's where I always hear it, in the wall."

Tad has moved right next to the wall and is feeling along each crack and crevice. "Any idea how it might have gotten in?"

"Who knows," she says. "An old thing like this. I was wanting them to take it down, but my son said he wouldn't have a place for the mower if they did that."

Tad taps the wall—not even trying to hide it. I guess he doesn't have to since we're pest control now. It rings like a hollow door. "Man, no insulation," Tad says, and I notice that he's a better actor than I am. "We'll bring someone out later today to open up this wall and spray."

"Oh, thank goodness," the woman says. "It's been weeks." I realize then that I'd be a terrible landlord because I'm not sure I could handle people calling and complaining all the time and saying the same things over and over.

A car pulls into the driveway. "Oh," she says. "My

son. I called him about my dog. If you two see a poodle wandering anywhere, please bring it back. He just ran off this morning."

I notice the beat-up truck, the gun rack in the bed, and not to profile or anything, but this guy steps out of the truck wearing a camo shirt and jacket, and I remember that I'm in a cardigan and Tad has a cane, and we don't look too much like pest specialists.

"You know, you go talk to him while we check a few more things," I say. "We'll just let ourselves out when we're done."

Tad is holding his phone like he's dying to call Anderson.

"Let me, uh, text our boss too," I say. "He'll want to come out when we open up this wall."

"Just don't damage it too much," she says. "My son tells me it helps keep the kitchen warm to have it there."

Tad nods. I text. The woman leaves. And I hate to say it like this, but we're a little trapped here.

"Did you text Anderson?" Tad asks.

I nod.

"We better bolt as soon as they go inside."

Through a little crack between the doors, I can see that the son is smoking and she's talking to him outside, waiting for him to finish the cigarette. "Oh no," I say.

Tad nods, smelling the air again. "As soon as she tells him we're going to take the wall out today, we'll lose a lot of our evidence."

"What do you mean?" I ask.

"I'll tell you if we ever get out of here."

The butt of the man's cigarette burns orange against the gray sky. Almost gone. I can't hear what she says through the fresh pattering of rain, but I see it on his face—a quick shot of anger, smoothed over with worry.

I can see her try to reassure him, reach out for his arm. He brushes her away. *Please go inside,* I think, but he's coming here, this direction, straight for the shed.

Tad hears the footfalls, even with the rain, but I'm guessing he doesn't see what I can see—the handgun strapped to a holster around the man's waist.

"Macie," he whispers. "What kind of truck is that?"

"Blue GMC," I say. "Don't ask me for the year because I'm not good at that stuff."

"Shhhh," he says, even though I'm whispering.

"What do you want to do?" I murmur.

"We need to leave," he says, "as soon as possible." But at that moment, the door creaks open.

I get a quick glance at the hairy, pocked hands before Tad grabs my waist and pulls me in tight, pressing his mouth to mine. It's warm, hot—or maybe that's just me. But not soft like I'd imagined it to be—tight, tense. A sliver of light widens as the door opens and Tad pushes harder. I want to gasp, but find that any air I ever had in my body has left me.

Suddenly, Tad jerks back. "Oh, hey man. Wow. Oh, I'm sorry. We were just checking out the pests."

He grabs my wrist and pulls me toward the door, stumbling down the little ledge of a step, but that's okay, because it makes the act look that much more real.

"I mean, whoa, that's embarrassing. A little unprofessional, I know. Just don't tell the owner, okay. We'll grab our boss and be back later to take care of that pest problem. She thinks it's in the wall, but I'm pretty sure it's the floor. Course we got a little distracted looking. Boss'll find out for sure."

In about two minutes (though it feels like a hundred years), we're back in my car.

Tad sinks his head down on the dash and I start the car.

"What was THAT?" I ask.

"Hopefully an amazing distraction," Tad replies. "Do you think he noticed our clothes? Too bad I couldn't have gotten your cardigan off, that would have made it look even more legit."

"You mean insane," I say, turning even redder than I already am.

"Look, Macie, I'm really sorry—that was super out of line, but it was all I could think of. I just had a second. We needed something to distract him from how we look."

I know I'm distracted, but I have no idea about the guy. I can't even picture his face. I can't do anything but taste Tad's lips—the after-flavor of him. Although I shake it off, all wrong—from the haste to the hardness to the...I lick my lips again.

We peel into the street and the guy is already moving the mower out of the shed. His mother is calling to him from the back door, holding a cup of steaming coffee in her hands. He looks at it, then walks over under the awning and takes it, sipping, staring.

"We've got to get Anderson here as soon as possible," Tad is saying, like he's forgotten he shoved me into a kiss.

I'm stuck in kissing loop and can't think straight. How long were we there? Why wasn't it softer?

"That guy's going to remove all the evidence as soon as he can," Tad says.

"What evidence?" I ask, touching my face, which is so hot from embarrassment and who knows what else that I feel like it's going to ignite any minute.

"That guy's been hiding something in that shed. At night. Then closing up the wall. I'd bet a million dollars it's drugs. But it'll all be gone if we don't hurry."

"Tad," I start again, tapping my lips.

"And," he interrupts. "That truck. It was the same make of truck that Officer Petersburg stopped. Did you catch the license plate?"

Right now I'm barely catching anything. I stare through the drizzle, trying to picture it. "Maybe," I say. I see the blue paint, scraped at the back, just under the GMC symbol. The bumper, a little bent. SAJ2... And then I lose it, or at least I'm not sure about it.

I blow out a hot breath. "This is not how I planned to spend my day. Finding a dead couple's dog, faking pest control, running from a dangerous guy after..."

"Macie, I'm really sorry," Tad interrupts. "It was just—all I could think to do."

I have to admit that the idea of kissing Tad has taken a portion of my thinking space as well these last few weeks, but I have a feeling that's not what he means.

"All you could think to do?" I ask.

"Don't tell Sal."

"We broke up." From a relationship that never really existed.

"Oh, right. At least I won't get a fist in my face then."

"Oh, don't worry," I say, taking a deep breath and circling back through the neighborhood, wondering what that guy is doing. "That kiss was all for work so I'm sure he'd be cool with it even if we were together."

"I'm sorry, Macie. It wasn't right of me. I just, what else should I have done?"

I don't know. Anything. It's like a fantasy dream that goes all wrong at the end.

"Did you just turn left?" Tad asks.

"Yeah, I'm circling back to see what he's doing."

"Macie, we need to get Anderson."

"You said yourself that we have to hurry if we want to catch this guy, or get evidence of something."

"They'll know there's been meth there," he says.

"If I'm right. They can test the buildings. We just won't have anything to prove it was him."

"Great," I say, as I turn another corner. The rain picks up again, hitting the windshield in bursts. "Then you can just sit here and make out with me while I get some pictures." I park and jerk off my cardigan so I'll be a little less recognizable.

"Macie," he says. "I can tell you're mad, and I'm sorry."

"I'm not mad," I say, which might be a small bit of a lie. "You've got to do what you've got to do."

"I'm not doing that again," he says.

"Why not?" I ask, so disconnected from my feelings that I don't even know what's going on in my body. "You just did it once."

"But I barely knew what I was doing. Something just kicked in and I did it. I can't just do it now. Not with you so tense and angry like that."

"Like what?" I say, looking down and getting out my phone. "Just one kiss. I'm sure you can do it. And if Rebecca's mad, well, I won't tell."

"Rebecca?" he asks, then. "Oh. She was just my date. It wasn't anything. I mean, she's nice, but…"

He can't finish because I'm leaning over toward him. I've got my camera in hand behind his back, pointed out the window. "Go on," I say.

He looks at me, that eye, the pinprick of vision. What is he seeing? "No, I can't."

And can't he? Why not? I jerk him toward me in a gesture that feels rough just as an explosion of some sort goes off. Tad pins me down in the car, his body on top of mine, his arms wrapped around me, both of us breathing, hearts racing, terror not passion, a Picasso of a love story. A shot. From the shed.

Silence follows. One minute, then another. My heart pounds against the pounding of Tad's heart. I can feel the tight sinews of his biceps pinning me down, the ripples of chest underneath his shirt. But also… The edge of the seatbelt pokes into my back so hard that I almost want to cry, and we're both sweating like hogs. Romantic stuff. Sirens are pouring through the air, warping and shattering against the sounds of pounding rain. Tad breathes deeply and kind of leans his forehead against mine and for a minute I don't really care that I'm being speared with a seatbelt or that I probably have armpit stains that could compete with Sylvester Stallone on *Rocky IV*. But I remember that forced kiss—that we've-got-to-escape-kiss, and I take a deep breath, exhale out my fluster. "What's happening?" I whisper, my lips almost brushing Tad's cheek.

He swallows, and I'm close enough that I can feel it. It suddenly feels stupidly embarrassing and I have to resist the urge to shove him off of me. "There's a SWAT team," he says. "I'm not sure if that guy shot himself or at the cops. But they've surrounded that shed."

"Guess I should have brought snacks," I say from beneath the man who's occupied more than one just-before-sleep thought in my mind over the last few weeks.

Tad laughs, and it's a good sound. "Yeah," he says. "This could take hours. I could really use some of those cheese and peanut butter crackers right now."

I giggle and he slips an arm under my back and then sort of props himself up on his other elbow, his eyes an inch from my face. I know he can see me. "Macie," he says.

Another shot, and Tad pushes back down, his skin against mine, cheek to cheek, his arm around my back. I can feel sweat dripping down my neck, seeping through my clothes. It feels like the most embarrassing moment ever.

Then the announcement from the megaphone. Nelson's voice—a rich chocolate—probably good at soothing dangerous criminals threatening to blow up buildings or victims or their own heads.

It's over. The guy must have come out. Tad sits up, ever so slightly, trying to help me up while staying low. It's not a graceful event on my part. I wiggle and jerk, so that I can get to a place where I can discreetly peek through the window. They're cuffing the guy, reading his rights, leading him into the back of one of the cars. The old woman is bawling her brains out as Anderson talks to her, probably getting a statement, and a bunch of other cops are taping off the area.

"Macie," Tad asks. "What's going on? Sum it up for me; I'm having trouble catching all of it. They've got the guy."

"Yeah," I say, then fill him in on the other details.

"Is anyone hurt?"

"Doesn't look like it," I answer. "But when everyone's distracted, we should leave. They could take forever with the statement from the renter and my neck is going to cramp into uncontrollable spasms at any moment."

The cop car with the bad guy rolls away and there's enough bustle that now seems like the time. "Come on."

I whip on my seat belt, only slightly aware that I'm still sweating buckets, like I'm in the middle of hot yoga, not my car on a cool fall day.

Tad is still scrunched down low, peering out the window, though I'm not sure how much he can see.

When we get to the station, waiting for Anderson in my car, I kind of want to laugh and cry and maybe scream a little too. Tad looks at me, squeezes my sweaty arm. "When Anderson gets here, we'll be able to tell him what we know."

"Okay," I say, looking down at my muddy clothes, then digging around in my console for a tissue to towel off my face. Tad pulls out a handkerchief (of course he does), and I'm just left being the most backwoods kid in town. I can taste the salt from the sweat on my lips. "You head in," I say. "Just give me a second to try to clean up."

"Great work, Mace," he replies, reaching for his cane, making his way out of the car like he didn't just sweat the Atlantic Ocean while being pinned under his secret crush. Oh, that's right, because he didn't.

My mascara has run. It's the only makeup I'm wearing and it couldn't even come through for me and not leave me looking like Creepy the Clown. The pits of my blouse are hosting broad, round sweat stains. I dig around on the floor for my cardigan and find it—mud from one of my feet smeared along the right side—so that can't save me. The mud doesn't stop at my sweater either. I notice that I've also got a smeared footprint on my pant leg and a little between my nails. I look like a criminal more than someone who could apprehend one. Even if I could find a tissue or wipe in my car, it would never be enough to solve the problem that is me right now. My house is ten minutes away. Ten minutes from a shower and some clean clothes and a modicum of non-disgustingness. I turn on the engine and peel out.

Thirty minutes later, when I get back, Tad is ticked. "Where were you? Everything's a hot mess here and we needed you. Where's that dog? I couldn't even remember the guy's name."

"It's the humane society," I say. "Pretty basic. And I thought you had a photographic memory anyway."

"It's been a distracting day," he says.

And he could definitely say that again.

"I had to get cleaned up," I mutter.

"You looked fine," he says.

"I looked like I'd spent the morning dumpster diving," I answer, just as Anderson walks in.

"Well, look who decided to show up," he says.

"You caught the guy," I reply.

"No thanks to you," he says.

I admit that I'm a little confused. Does he mean, *All thanks to you,* because I'm pretty sure that's what he should mean. "We found the dog," I say. "And the shed. Tad called you a bazillion times."

"He called once; texted once. As did you," Anderson corrects. "And I was dealing with some things. Like apprehending the guy who shot Officer Petersburg."

It takes me a second.

Anderson helps me out. "Tad claims he's also the Samuelson killer."

I nod stupidly while my brain catches up, piecing the details together. So this guy's running a meth lab out of Mom's shed. But then—when the landlord goes to check on a supposed pest problem —the landlord finds out, maybe threatens to call the cops. So guy follows him home, sneaks up behind him, shoots him dead with his right hand, but the wife is there too. She comes in, freaks out. That's a problem. Or is it? Because she provides an opportunity for the killer to look innocent—if he can shoot her from the same place the husband was standing, if he can leave the gun in the dead husband's hand, then this whole thing will shake down like a good old-fashioned murder-suicide. But then there was this dog. He could have killed it too, but that would have looked more suspicious, so he takes the dog, gives it to Mom—what a guy. Then it's back to business as usual. Back to scratching around at night, worrying his mom over her "raccoon" problem. And then a misstep. He goes too fast on the road, and he's got something in his car. When the friendly traffic officer comes over and asks him to step out, boom, out comes the gun. Off goes the car, back to Mom's house. Two weirdos making out in the shed—hopefully Tad left out that detail. But the cops have managed to track him, find him. Then just as we're leaving, things go wild.

"But I'm going to need some proof," Anderson is saying. "More than a meth lab. That just means he's a dealer like we thought."

"The dog is at the humane society," I say. "My friend John is keeping him. Even if the woman won't testify, he's got her name as someone who was looking for the dog—a dog she got from her son just two and a half weeks ago. John wrote it all down. He's good about that stuff."

"That meth head could have just found that dog wandering," Anderson says.

"Didn't," I answer.

"But could have. It's still not solid evidence."

"What about the gun?" Tad asks.

"Unregistered," Anderson answers. "Could have been anyone's."

"More likely to be a criminal's," Tad says.

"Yes, but still circumstantial," Anderson answers.

And then, I remember something. Hands. Something I notice, something I know. "You'll find the killer's blood on Phillip Samuelson's clothes."

"How so? There was a lot of blood on Samuelson's clothes."

"Exactly," I say, "which is why nobody thought about it, why the killer himself wouldn't have noticed."

"Where?" Anderson asks.

"Probably a sleeve, along the cuff."

"Why?"

"Because the dog bit the killer. After that the killer must have locked it in a room or something. But when he put the gun in Phillip's hand, a little of his own blood would have brushed the cuff."

"You've been reading too many detective novels," Anderson says, but he's listening; I can tell he's listening.

"It was two and a half weeks ago, so the killer wouldn't have a big wound left to show for it, not even real scratches, but when someone gets scratched or cut or bitten and their skin heals, it's a little lighter, a little pinker."

I grab my notebook from my desk, start to sketch them out. "When I saw his hand, I thought they were freckles or pockmarks at first, but he had four pink dots on the side of his hand, near his wrist. Dots of healed skin from a dog bite." I hold up the paper. It's hastily drawn, but from the look on Anderson's face, I can tell that he gets the idea.

He turns on his heel. Not even a 'Good work, Greene.' But with Anderson, I'm pretty sure that silence is exactly what that means.

———

And I'm right. On Monday, instead of closing the case and leaving it as a murder-suicide, Anderson tells me they found blood from the killer—Harold Rackman—on Phillip Samuelson's sleeve, and the remnant of a wound on Rackman's hand, a bite mark that perfectly matches Bernard's brave mouth. The old woman is willing to testify when it comes up in court, so John's statement isn't quite as vital, but they still ask him several questions about dog bites and warn him he may be called to testify in court.

"You've added some excitement to my life," John says when I call to ask how Bernard is doing. "A little too much, truth be told."

We both laugh.

"And Bernard's doing great," he says. "If no one from the family wants to take him, he'll be adopted in a flash. For now, I've been taking him to my house for some special treatment."

"Oh John, you're the best."

"Was that ever a question?"

few days later, Tad shows up on my doorstep. He doesn't even let me invite him in before blurting, "Macie, about that case, the shed and all—I know you're still mad and I'm really sorry."

"Hey," I say. "No big deal. You did what you had to do and it worked out." I'm not even lying—not too much anyway—about it not being a big deal.

"Yeah," he says, shifting like he's going to leave, but then tapping his way inside my house and to my couch.

"So this feels super awkward, especially since I can tell from your voice that you're still a little bugged—" he starts.

"—But I'm not," I interrupt. Surely I don't sound bugged, not that much anyway.

He responds by setting his cane on the floor. "Listen, I've been thinking about the whole thing."

"Yeah, me too," I say. "And Tad, just forget it. It was an accident, or a necessity, or something like that, and it's over."

"Honestly, I wasn't worrying, just…"

I notice that his Uber is waiting outside, so he didn't intend for this to be a long visit. "You can let it go," I say. "We did an awesome job, nailed a bad guy. We're a good team."

"We are," he says, leaning forward. The lights are dim in the living room and I wonder how it affects his vision.

"And I just," he says, "I don't want you to be angry about it. I'm really sorry. More sorry than you know."

"Don't worry," I repeat. He obviously feels terrible and any lingering annoyance I might have had melts away. "Just forget it ever happened."

"Yeah," he says. "But the thing is…" From the front window I can see that his Uber guy is checking his watch.

"You better get going," I say. "Your driver will charge you a fortune."

"Yeah," Tad mumbles. "Wouldn't want that." He takes his cane and stands, tapping his way forward, shoulders square and beautiful.

I don't know why I want to run after him, but it's definitely my impulse. As with many of my impulses, I turn around and shut the door on it. Then lean against it, like I'm holding it shut against an intruder. My face is sweating again, my neck, just like it did that day. But I refuse to think about it. Will. Not. Think. About. It.

We're a good team, and there's no way on earth I'm going to ruin that.

CHAPTER 34

Gretchen calls me on Friday. "Hey, girl, how'd the lipstick work out for that gala? Hope it got some good use."

The gala seems like forever and ever ago, but I realize it was just one little week. And, if by *use*, she means that I reapplied it after I ate, then, yes, it got great use. "It looked awesome," I say.

"And…" she prods.

"And it didn't get smeared all over my date's face."

"Hmmm," she says. "Sounds like a date that didn't work out."

I laugh. "It worked out how it was supposed to."

"Then are you maybe up for lunch tomorrow?"

"Sure," I say.

"Let's meet at the Italian one near the mall. I'm off at one."

"Works for me."

"Also, I don't exactly read the papers, but a little bird told me your name was in it."

"In the newspaper?" I ask.

"Yeah, the cop section was pretty loaded this week, I guess. You're kind of a hero."

I think of the kiss with Tad and I don't feel like a hero.

"Anyway, I can't wait to hear about it. See you tomorrow."

I set my phone down just as it dings with a text. This one is Rebecca. "You feeling better after last week?"

It takes me a minute to figure out what she's talking about. Oh yeah, again with the gala. Me rushing off.

"Yeah, great," I type back.

"And Sal? How are things?"

"He's fine. I'm fine."

She sends an emoji with the eyebrow raised.

"We weren't the right fit." Just like I'm not the right fit with anyone. But I don't say that part. What I do say is that she should come for lunch with me and Gretchen. "She's the one who sells the lipstick."

"Well then I'm in."

And you know, I never would have said that I was good at the girl date thing, but even stone cold sober, we're laughing our heads off before the appetizers arrive. Gretchen is regaling us with some story about a customer getting stuck in a swimsuit and needing her help to get it off. I'm telling them about the fake pest control bit and almost getting caught by the perpetrator. They're giggling and digging for more details, but when Rebecca asks, "How'd you two get out of it?" I sort of skip the kissing part and tell them Tad stumbled down the step as a distraction and then we raced to the car.

"Honestly, if the cops hadn't come, who knows what would have happened. I'm not sure they would have caught the guy. He was about to get rid of as much evidence as he could and make a break for it."

"That poor dog," Rebecca coos. "Do you know what happened to it?"

"It'll go up for adoption after the trial—if John hasn't gotten too connected to it, that is. Who knows, maybe it'll go back to the old lady."

"You sure she's innocent?" Gretchen asked. "Maybe she's just a crazy boss lady running a meth lab and her son is just another one of her pawns."

I think about the forty thousand phone calls she

left after the couple got shot. "Nah," I say. "I think she's clean. And she could use a dog in her life with her son gone. Everybody needs a little companionship."

"Which reminds me," Rebecca says, leaning forward. She's wearing one of the samples Gretchen gave her and it looks completely amazing and she should definitely buy it. "Since things with Sal are over, is there anything…else…going on?"

I look to the left, sip my lemonade. "Nah," I say. "Just hanging out with you hooligans."

"And I mean, that's definitely the right choice," Gretchen says.

"But we're not going to do you much good when the nights get cold," Rebecca adds.

"I like the cold," I reply.

"Of course you do," Gretchen says, laughing.

Rebecca lets out an exasperated sigh. "Come on, there's got to be something between you and Tad."

And, I'm not going to lie, the comment catches me off guard. I might blush a little. I try my hardest not to, but it's kind of like trying to control breathing or something. It doesn't usually work out great. "What?" I ask, stalling.

"You two," she says. "I saw you dance."

"We're just work partners," I reply.

She cocks an eyebrow. "He talked about you the

whole night. But it was cute—like he kept trying not to and then talking about you anyway. And then you left. I thought there might have been a thing."

The way she says it she means, *There was definitely a thing.*

"There's not a thing."

"You sure?" she asks.

"Yeah," I say, thinking of that hard kiss, of Tad's face in the car. "We just work really well together."

That eyebrow of hers springs up again, but she doesn't say anything else and our meals arrive to save me. At least for a minute.

"Maybe there should be a thing," she says, and Gretchen demands a picture.

Rebecca pulls one up of Tad and her at the gala and I shove food in my face until Gretchen squeals, "Not bad. Why don't *you* go after him, Becca, if Macie won't?"

I listen closely, waiting for her answer.

"I'm like his kid sister. And, like I said, he talked about Macie the whole night."

More food into my endless maw.

"Macie," Gretchen says. "He's so hot. Why wouldn't you make a play for him?"

"I'm not really the make-a-play type." That's true enough.

"Do you really not like him?" Rebecca asks.

"I like him," I answer. "We work great together."

"She likes him," Gretchen says.

"So what's wrong?" Rebecca says.

"We work really well together," I repeat.

Gretchen nods slowly. "Yeah, it could get awkward, I guess."

Rebecca isn't giving in to me yet. That eyebrow is up again.

"You know," I say to Rebecca, diverting the conversation. "Your sister indirectly gave us one of the clues for the case."

And then I tell them about the dog bark and how we'd been talking about the YouTube channel and then we watch one of Becca's sister's videos together and Gretchen gets teary over it and our dessert arrives, and it's the most fun I've had in a long, long time.

At the end of lunch, the girls hug me. I'm not a huge hugger, but maybe it's time to start. "You're a hero," Gretchen says as we leave.

I'm not sure I've ever been a hero. Dental receptionists usually aren't, though I know I was a hero to Rachel and Aiden, because friends are always heroes to each other. After Rachel died, I always wondered if I'd find someone to take her place. Which was the wrong way to think, because I won't. But maybe, maybe I can find people to be my friends.

We agree to go ice skating the next weekend. Ice skating. Like we're a bunch of tweens. Except there's a happy hour.

"Are you guys crazy?" I ask. "I'm not drinking and skating."

Rebecca snorts out a laugh, tucking the lipstick she's bought into her purse.

"Then eat wings and skate. It's going to be fun."

I'm not even sure wings and skating are a good idea for me, but somehow it sounds fun anyway. A lot of fun.

On the way home, I catch myself thinking of my ex. All these months I've missed Rachel, missed friendship. But I never once missed Alex (though I did miss his meals). I never once wondered if I'd find anyone to take Alex's place—why would I have wanted that? Maybe what he thought about me was right—I'm just not the romance type. Too boring, too basic, too…me. Good friend, good listener, hearer, seer. But I'm not hot, and I'm awkward and practical and the type of girl guys kiss for a ruse and nothing else. For Alex, I was the stable one, and when he got tired of stability, he got tired of me. For Tad, well, I'm just his partner in crime (ha, see what I did there). And I guess that's good enough.

A little idea creeps into my head, a gift I should get Tad, something that says, "Hey, it's okay."

On the way home, I stop at a Hallmark shop, something I've done all of never times in my life. But they've got what I need—walls of cards. I find the one I want. It costs almost $10, and that is exactly why I've never stopped at this store on the way home, but I fork over the money, and the deed is done.

What is it, you ask, this thing that is worth such moral compromise on my part as to fork out ten dollars for a piece of paper? A pop-up card of a poodle, that's what. Now I just have a little crafting left to do. I'm not any kind of crafter, but fortunately for this sort of project, I don't need mad skills.

CHAPTER 35

Monday comes like Mondays do, and I glance sideways to Tad's desk a thousand times before he finally notices the little envelope, almost starts with surprise as his fingers run over it. That alone was worth the money. He doesn't open it, though, not there. Instead, he takes the card, along with his lunch, and makes his way out of the office—not to his usual haunt at the bench in the courtyard. In fact, I have no idea where he goes. It takes literally all my willpower not to get up and follow him. Instead, I take my own lunch to the courtyard, hoping to see him.

It's a full hour before that happens. My sandwich is ancient history and I'm back at my desk sketching hands before he returns. I look for the card, and it's there, in his hand. No word about it though. Not till the end of the day when most people are emptying out and I'm gathering up my things.

"Hey Macie," he starts.

"Did you like the card?" I pipe up, not able to wait a single second longer. "Just a little something to commemorate the case. Our first."

A beat before he answers, but I know he liked the card; how could he not? It's hilarious.

He's smiling, in weird way.

"You could tell what it was, right?" I ask the question before thinking that maybe it's rude.

"Yeah," he says. "A pop-up card of a dog."

"Could you see the rest of it?"

"Yeah," he says, but his voice is slow, like he's looking for the right words.

"You didn't think it was funny?"

His fingers tap along the edge of the envelope and I have to tap away the thought of how those fingers would feel tapping along me.

"Man's best friend," he says. "With your face glued on the card."

"Funny, right?" I say, digging a little harder this time.

"Sure," he says, but it doesn't sound sure.

I deflate a little. If I can't even be funny; if he can't even laugh at the card.

"It was sweet of you, Macie," he's saying, then

more throat clearing. "You know, I was thinking we should go back to that diner sometime. You liked the pie, right?"

"Definitely," I say, trying to clear the feeling up between us. A nice friend date at the greasy spoon. "Maybe for lunch tomorrow."

"Okay," he says, though he sounds a bit defeated. "That'd be nice. And I'll pay."

I laugh. "Should be cheap, cause I think I'm just going pie."

Having Tad as my friend makes three. Three friends, plus Aiden and Gabby, bringing it up to five. I mean, not bad for me. Not bad at all.

My father was never much of a gambler, but once, during a heated game of Jenga (in which I may or may not have thrown a huge fit and accused him of cheating when everything came tumbling down), he told me, "At gambling, the deadly sin is to mistake bad play for bad luck."

I always played Jenga the same. It was a safe way. I'd follow the exact same pattern when I removed the blocks. I liked patterns, and they usually came through for me. Usually. But sometimes, even when something felt a little shaky, even when my gut told me to try a different tactic, I'd still take those blocks out in that same pattern. But that day, it gave my dad an advantage. Because he'd already made a tricky move, removed a risky block. Which meant that when I went for my usual play—boom—they'd all come crashing down.

I feel like I'm there again, playing Jenga with my dad. Things still look stable.

After all, everything that was wrong is now right. We've solved the case, found the dog, cleared Phil Samuelson's name. Anderson's happy. Chief is beaming. Life is good. Macie and I are cool again. Friends.

I could keep going, follow my pattern. A little snark, a little savvy, a greasy diner for lunch. That type of play. It's safe.

Until, of course, it isn't.

Because I know deep down that things are shaky. I can feel the emptiness of that Jenga tower, the gentle sway. I can feel something in my gut telling me to deviate from my pattern, my usual course. There's another piece at the corner of the tower. Removing it will be a risk. It could bring the whole thing down. Or. It could be the move that lets me win, that keeps the tower up for my turn, but makes it too unstable for my dad's.

"The deadly sin is to mistake bad play for bad luck."

Which will it be—the safe move, or the risky one?

CHAPTER 36

The next day Tad texts me that he won't be at work because he's busy with something. "No worries," I text back and I mean it.

Sal is chatting it up with a new cop who has just joined us—a lady cop, as my mama would have said, though I wouldn't. But she's young and pretty and she seems tough as nails. Shouldn't be too long before she's the one getting flowers on her desk. Which will give me one more friend: Sal. Not bad.

For just a flash, I picture my lonely house. No one to come home to, but it's been that way for a while, so it shouldn't feel any lonelier now, right? Especially when the week has been so full. I realize that that's exactly the problem. I wish I had someone to talk to about it. And ever since my fake kiss with Tad, I can't help but think that I wouldn't mind having someone to do more than talk with. But that's a wish for another day, maybe another lifetime.

I swing by the humane society on my way home from work, check in with John, ask about Bernard. Apparently, he's doing so well that he might not be up for adoption after the trial. "You're keeping him?" I ask.

"We've grown attached," John says. "I can usually keep a little distance; otherwise, I'd be running a total zoo in my house, but that guy, he's such a sweetheart. And his owner's dead, and the old woman who cared for him is unable to get him back until after the trial, if then. It just got me."

I nod as we wander along the cages. There's a new batch of kittens nursing, snuggling and wiggling at their mother's belly. Along with a fat white rabbit with pink eyes that honestly creep me out just a little. Two lizards. "Those are new," I say.

"You into reptiles?" he asks.

"Not at all."

We wander into the room that used to have the kittens that cuddled into my lap—the ones who helped me figure out a part of the case—but only two are left. The Orange and Spider are gone. "Oh," I say, except that I really just mouth it because I'm so disappointed that no sound comes out. I clear my throat. "Did those two get adopted?"

"Just today," John says, looking away. "I'm sorry. You never called to tell me you wanted one."

I didn't, but I wanted both of them. Though, to be fair, I didn't fully realize it until this moment. Until they were gone and I couldn't get them back. Are we noticing a theme here? "Well, if it doesn't work out with the new owner, will you give me a call then?" I say.

"Sure, Macie," John says, like it's probably going to work out with the new owner, so I shouldn't get my hopes up. "Got that new batch though."

"Yeah," I say, but they're still nursing and the truth is I don't really want to look today. Don't want to keep thinking about doing things I don't do. Don't want to realize I want something only when it's finally gone.

I need to call Tad.

*I*nstead, I end up swinging by his house. Great idea, right?

Wrong.

He comes to the door after a bit of a wait. I can hear him banging around inside and shutting doors and stuff, so I know he's home. Then he shows up like I've never seen him, shirt hanging out like he just threw it on.

"Oh, hey," I say. "I was just driving home and thought I'd stop by to see if you were okay. Since you were sick today and all." He doesn't look sick. Disheveled, yes. Sick, not at all.

"I wasn't sick," he says. "Just busy."

"Oh," I say. "Okay."

There's a bit of sound from the bedroom and I look toward the door, the closed door, then back at Tad with his untucked shirt, the shirt that it looks like he just threw on. Oh no.

"Actually I have a something going on right now," Tad is saying.

· I hear a bit of a scuffle in his bedroom, and something falls to the floor. Yup, I bet he does. And here I am late late late to the party again. "Oh, hey, no problem. I'll just catch you later."

"Yeah, maybe—could I stop by tonight? I've got a thing for you."

"Oh, yeah, sure." Great. A reciprocal gift because I gave him that card. Awesome. And I thought we were past that. I thought… Well, who even knows what I thought. I thought I didn't need something until that something was gone. All the somethings apparently. But things don't wait forever. Not kittens, and definitely not men.

"Great, Macie," Tad says, and he's inching the door closed on me.

And wouldn't it be wild and non-basic if I shoved that door back open and marched in and wrapped him up in a steaming hot kiss. Yes, yes it would. But he's legit got another woman with him, and non-basic or not, that just wouldn't be cool. Even less cool than stealing someone's kittens.

"See you tonight, Macie."

"Yeah," I say. "I'll, um, be around." Of course I will.

I go home, start my mail delivery dinner. Tonight it's scallops and veggies. I'm not a big scallop person, but if Alex could do it, then so can I. If I was cool, I'd have some bottle of wine I could pop open somewhere, but since I'm me, I think the best I have is some frozen grape juice concentrate. It'll have to do.

I'm just about to mix up my juice when the doorbell rings.

Tad stands there, a box in his arms. "Hey, Mace."

"Hey," I say, eyeing the box suspiciously. It's way bigger than a pop-up card.

"Can I come in?" he asks.

"Sure. I've got some dinner going."

I think I hear this little squeak, but I have to rush into the kitchen to make sure the scallops aren't overcooking. If they do, they'll taste like rubber, and even lonely single ladies don't like rubber for dinner.

Tad sets the box down and follows me in, sniffing. "Smells divine, Macie. Didn't know you were a whiz in the kitchen too."

I nod to the packaging, then say, "Delivery service. They do all the work. I put it on the stove. Not much whizzery about it."

"Still better than I could do," Tad says, stepping closer.

The dinner is made for two. I usually just save the leftovers for the next day, but scallops will just taste fishy. "Do you want some?"

"Oh, no. I don't want to eat your dinner."

"It's more than I can eat."

He sniffs again. "Are you sure?"

Guess his lady friend from earlier doesn't…I stop on the thought. It's stupid and mean anyway. "I'm sure. It'll be done in just a couple minutes. Hopefully I didn't let the scallops go rubbery."

"Oh," he says. "Your present. Let me know when you're ready for it." He cocks his head to the side. "It's ready for you."

I toss in another pat of butter just for good measure, then sweep the pan off the stove. "Don't you think we should eat first? It'll go cold pretty quick."

Tad deliberates for a second, still leaning toward the front room where he's left the box. "It'll only take a minute," he says. "Let me get it."

He slips away and I get down two plates, a couple wine glasses even though there's still no wine, and a bar of dark chocolate I've been saving. I don't know why. Tad's just a friend from work, that's all. No need to pull out all the stops, right? But I haven't had a proper guest in forever, and honestly it's kind of fun to have someone to share my meal for two with.

He wanders back in, stepping carefully with the box in his hands. It really is huge. I turn to get forks; and then the box meows.

I stop mid-motion—drawer open, hand poised above it. "Did that box just…meow?"

Tad's grinning this huge, ridiculous grin. "You'll have to open it and find out."

I turn, cutlery completely forgotten. He gestures to a chair at my own table, sets the box on my thighs. And, I don't know what's come over me, but my hands are completely shaking.

The box is unmistakably meowing now and I look up at him before folding back the flaps. And there they are. The little orange and her naughty brother. For a moment, I just stare. Maybe I breathe; I can't be sure. And then, well, I start to cry, sob actually.

It's apparently not the response that Tad was looking for. And I get it. I mean, normally, I'm not the crying type. I cried when Rachel died. I even cried when I got divorced, though not as much. But normally it's just not my thing. It's just that this last week—it's been so awkward. Tad not liking the card, then the thing at his house. And me, just drawing hands. Just coming home to no one. The tears pour out of my eyes.

Tad gropes for a chair, sits down. "Oh, hey. It's okay. I, um, I went to that animal shelter and the guy in charge, he said these were up for adoption, and I don't know what it was about them, but they just kind of hooked me and maybe it was stupid, but I thought—"

He stops, then starts again. "Look, it's okay if you don't want them. I checked with that guy—John. You can bring them back if it doesn't work out. I can take them back first thing tomorrow."

The way he says it, I can tell that the thought of returning them breaks his heart.

I try to tell him, 'No, of course, don't take them back,' but all that comes out of my blubbering mouth is "No."

"Okay, okay. I'll just..." He tries to take the box, but I cling onto it, holding it close to my chest.

Then Tad sniffs. The vegetables are burning. I set

the box down, rush to the oven, open the door, whip out crispy brown broccoli florets.

When I turn back to him, he's tickling the orange on the chest. I almost start to blubber again, especially with that smell of burned broccoli.

"Or maybe I'll just have to keep them," he murmurs.

"Don't you dare," I say, finally shaking out of it, coming back to myself. I sweep the box with kittens out of his arms, ignoring my cold scallops, my blackened broccoli.

Tad is trying to take the kittens back to end this ridiculous scene and I can barely talk. All I say is, "I want them," and plunk the box on the table, scooping out the little orange, followed by the naughty one—Spider. Somewhere through my stupor, I manage a "thank you."

"Are you sure, Macie?" he asks. "This isn't quite how I pictured it."

And then, I don't know how it happened, but he's hugging me. His arms are so tight, like they could hold up a world, but not mine. He kissed me as a ruse.

"Macie," he's saying. "Macie, please stop crying."

Am I? I didn't realize I'd started again. And then, I can't. I don't even know why. I have everything I ever wanted—a good house, a job, my name in the paper, hero status at work. I even have five friends—that's like, a record. Plus, a silver dress and a red tube of lipstick. What more could any woman want?

"Macie," he murmurs, leaning down. His lips just above mine, his nose touching my face. Just like that night at the gala, that night I left because it felt so close, but too far. But this time, I don't run away. I feel his chest, the thunder of his heart. How did I not feel that before? His skin—soft lips, rough chin, just like a man should be. I close my eyes, trying to close away the pounding everywhere in my skin, though it just won't close. And then one of the kittens pops up between us. I start to giggle—from crying to laughing like I'm a thirteen-year-old girl and puberty isn't playing nice. And then his hands come to my cheeks and his lips come to my mouth. And there's no one here we're trying to trick. He sinks into me, and I'm holding two cats, but it doesn't matter. Forever and nothing at all, that's what the time feels like when he pulls away, still holding my cheeks. "Macie," he says.

I don't answer. Every word I've ever known has left my head.

"I tried to tell you, that day," he says. "I kissed you because it was all I could think to do. Because it was what I'd been thinking of doing for weeks. But Sal was there at first with roses and that tux and it seemed like you deserved a full guy like that, not some blind man; and you were so beautiful and soft at the gala and thinking about you with Sal I could barely sleep; and then he was gone, but we had a case, and then after I kissed you, you were so angry —I thought it must have been the worst thing for you."

There are words—they're battering against my brain. I try to gather a few. "I thought it was just work. That I was just work. That I didn't deserve anything romantic—that's how it always felt before in my life. Like I was just someone to pay the bills and make sure the shower got cleaned."

He moves a lock of hair off my face, takes Spider out of my arms and sets him on a kitchen chair. "Kissing you was the best work I've ever done in my whole life. If every minute of work could be like that…"

"But what about the woman?" I ask. "The one in your apartment today."

His forehead creases and he frowns.

"When I came by," I say. "I heard her."

"You heard her?" And then he laughs. "You mean the sounds from my bedroom? The moving and crashing. Think about it, Macie."

At that moment, Spider knocks a fork off the table. It clangs to the floor and Tad laughs again.

"You mean it was them?" I ask.

"Definitely no woman in my bedroom," he replies. "These guys would have gotten in the way anyway. Obviously."

He leans over the orange still in my arms and this time, I kind of jump toward it—the kiss. Again, like a thirteen-year-old girl. But Tad doesn't seem to mind. He presses his lips harder, then softer, in all the right combinations, teases his lips over my cheek. I'm pretty much ready to sink into his arms like a 1920s damsel when I notice Spider. He's on the table, eating scallops like it's his last meal and he's determined to make the most of it. Tad hears it just as I see it. And then we both laugh.

"Good thing you made that little prince dinner," Tad says. Then to the kitten, "Do you want her to keep you or not?"

"Pretty sure the food had gone cold anyway. And I definitely don't appreciate scallops the way he does."

"Although we better stop him or he'll wind up puking it all out." Tad scoops the naughty Spider into the crook of his elbow.

The orange has left my arms and is making her way more timidly, but with a certain amount of I-won't-be-left-out determination, toward the pan.

"You probably shouldn't let them learn to get on

the table and eat the food," Tad whispers, but neither of us makes a move to stop her. Not right now, on her first night here. Table training can come later. For now, she sticks a little paw into the pan, bats a scallop, then the scent overtakes her and she digs in.

I laugh, letting her eat one before grabbing her. "Thank you," I say. "I love them. How could you have possibly known?"

"I don't know," he says. "They just seemed like you. Besides, the day we were at that first apartment—our first case together with that dead guy—you just walking over to the kittens."

"Did I?" I ask.

"You did," he answers and leans down to kiss me again. In addition to his soft lips, I feel a little scratchy tongue at my arm and break away to see the orange grooming me.

"They're worse than kids," Tad says.

"Unlikely," I reply.

"What do you plan to name them?"

"Well, the dark one is Spider, obviously."

"Spider?"

"Yeah, he kept chasing a spider the first time we met, and it just fits. I've thought of him that way since then. But this girl..." I hold the orange out at arm's length. She gazes at me with those wide, green eyes. "Naming her Orange-y is a little too basic, even for me."

"Basic?" Tad asks.

"Yeah, boring," I say.

"I know what it means," he answers. "But you're hardly basic."

"I'm just a little plain."

"A woman who has a perfect memory for voices, a photographic memory for hands and faces. Someone who just solved a case and found a killer. Who impersonated a pest control company to do it. Nothing basic about that."

I laugh. And, I mean, it really isn't. Even if I do pay my bills and change my sheets regularly. "I guess," I say.

"I know," he replies, leaning his forehead against mine.

"Sunrise," I say suddenly.

"What?" he asks, tipping back.

"For the orange. Sunrise. My new beginning."

"I like it," he says.

"I love it," I reply and then jump toward him again, pressing my entire body into the kiss. The cats can eat every single scallop for all I care, lost in time, in the heat that comes from him and from my own pounding blood. Until the doorbell rings.

"You expecting anyone?" he asks.

I shake my head and try to ignore the door, though whoever it is rings again—a persistent two buzzes. When I tear myself away to open it, I see the Uber guy. I must be completely flushed because he looks me up and down like something's wrong with me. "Does your friend still want a ride?"

Tad walks up behind me, resting a soft hand on my shoulder. "Oh, man, so sorry."

"You forgot about me," the guy says.

"I'm really sorry," Tad says.

"It's okay," the guy says looking back and forth from me to Tad, "but you'll have to pay for all that time."

"Sure," Tad says, clicking his phone as the man leaves.

When the door is closed, he leans in again. "Back to business?" Then kisses my forehead, my cheek, my neck. Until we hear a scritch-scratch. "Litter box," Tad says, jumping back. "We better get it set up."

I'm ready to let everyone just poop on the floor, but Tad is hauling more things out of the box.

"We'll get things set up, and then... maybe...dinner?"

"Sounds amazing," I answer, though I'd definitely be happy to stay here all night too. But I guess a girl needs to have a little dignity.

"Where would you like to go?" he asks. "A greasy diner?" He smiles.

I wrinkle my nose, though I doubt Tad can see it. "You choose," I say. "Remember I'm basic. If you leave it up to me, we'll wind up at Olive Garden or something."

"Nothing wrong with that," he replies. "Though I might know a couple of other places."

He sweeps me up again and when I say 'sweeps,' I mean it really feels that way. He scoops me into his arms and my toes lift up off the floor. He pushes his nose to the right of mine and it's just the flush of my face burning into the softness of his cheek and I can't think of anything more airy than the feeling in my stomach, the lightness of his touch.

On the day of the trial, we make the nightly news. Okay, I don't, and there's a little side shot of Tad at his desk. So I should say that Anderson makes the news in a quick segment about the murder and car chase. In the reporting, they kind of blend the two events into one, like the news does. And it's not exactly that it wasn't one event—just not one that took place within the same twenty-four hour period.

Anderson does manage to mention his team, and how there's another dangerous criminal off the streets and on and on like Anderson does. I'm glad Tad made it into the frame and not me. He looks professional and handsome and better than the weird woman drawing in a lined notebook would have. But I know that notebook came in handy, along with, well, me.

A woman with five friends, and a boyfriend. Plus Anderson, I guess, and John definitely. Does that make it seven friends? Add to that two cats who positively adore my mail-in meals and act as little chaperones whenever Tad comes over. A circle of people (and animals) who love me, even with my quirks, maybe because of my quirks.

Tad was right—it's the least basic thing in the world.

ALSO BY J. E. PACE

From Ashes

Ready: A Short Prequel Story

Pulse: A Paramedic's Walk Along the Lines of Life and
Death

Also! If you enjoyed this book, **subscribe to my
newsletter**! You'll get the **prequel story, "Ready," for
FREE**, as well as updates on upcoming novels, sales, and
local events. You can subscribe HERE!

Looking for some stories about real life heroes? Check
out *Pulse: A Paramedic's Walk Along the Lines of Life and
Death*.

It's a collection of essays by my very own husband (his
stories, written by me) along with a few of my own essays,
which tell the spouse's side of the story.

ACKNOWLEDGMENTS

I always love the chance to thank the people who contributed to the book. First of all, a huge thank you to all the unsung heroes in our communities. In this book, I wanted to celebrate the police officers in our community and all those who help them.

Specifically, I'd like to thank Officers Jake and Brittni for their insights into police work. I asked them a bunch of questions as I wrote this, and they answered. I doubt I got every single detail right (in the cases where I didn't think to ask a question and should have), but the details I nailed are correct because of their help.

Additionally, I'd love to thank my wonderful editor, Carrie, who always cleans up my messes.

Finally, I want to thank my husband, Kip, and my kids for all the support they give me during a writing project.

ABOUT THE AUTHOR

J.E. Pace (who also writes under the name Jean Knight Pace) is the author of From Ashes and the short story, "Ready." Her other works include *Pulse: A Paramedic's Walk Along the Lines of Life and Death*, *Hugging Death: Essays on Motherhood and Saying Good-bye*, as well as *Four Seconds* (co-written with Laura Andrade). She lives in Indiana with her husband, four children, eight ducks, four chickens, and a cat. You can find more about her at jeanknightpace.com